PENGUIN BOOKS

MEMOIRS OF MANY IN ONE

Patrick White was born in England in 1912, when his parents were in Europe for two years; at six months he was taken back to Australia where his father owned a sheep station. When he was thirteen Patrick White was sent to school in England, to Cheltenham, 'where, it was understood, the climate would be temperate and a colonial acceptable'. Neither proved true, and after four rather miserable years there he went to King's College, Cambridge, where he specialized in languages. After leaving the university he settled in London, determined to become a writer. His first novel, *Happy Valley*, was published in 1939, and his second, *The Living and the Dead*, in 1941. Then during the war he was an R.A.F. Intelligence Officer in the Middle East and Greece. After the war he returned to Australia and is currently living in Sydney.

His other novels are *The Aunt's Story* (1946), *The Tree of Man* (1956), *Voss* (1957), *Riders in the Chariot* (1961), *The Solid Mandala* (1966), *The Vivisector* (1970), *The Eye of the Storm* (1973), *A Fringe of Leaves* (1976) and *The Twyborn Affair* (1979). In addition he has published two collections of short stories, *The Burnt Ones* (1964) and *The Cockatoos* (1974), which incorporates several short novels. His autobiography, *Flaws in the Glass*, was published in 1981. In 1973 he was awarded the Nobel Prize for Literature.

Memoirs of Many in One

By Alex Xenophon Demirjian Gray

EDITED BY
PATRICK WHITE

PENGUIN BOOKS

Penguin Books Ltd, Harmondsworth, Middlesex, England
Viking Penguin Inc., 40 West 23rd Street, New York, New York 10010, U.S.A.
Penguin Books Australia Ltd, Ringwood, Victoria, Australia
Penguin Books Canada Ltd, 2801 John Street, Markham, Ontario, Canada L3R 1B4
Penguin Books (N.Z.) Ltd, 182–190 Wairau Road, Auckland 10, New Zealand

First published in Great Britain by Jonathan Cape 1986
First published in the U.S.A. by Viking 1986
Published in Penguin Books 1987

Made and printed in Great Britain by
Richard Clay Ltd, Bungay, Suffolk
Typeset in Bembo

TO THE FLYING NUN

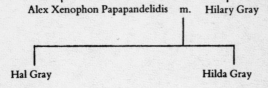

Stepho Papapandelidis m. Aliki Xenophon   Henry Gray m. Magda Demirjian

Alex Xenophon Papapandelidis   m.   Hilary Gray

Hal Gray   Hilda Gray

Editor's Introduction

After Mrs Gray's death I was asked by her daughter Hilda to edit the memoirs Alex had kept locked in a morocco writing case, behind arabesques in faded gilt, the work of some Turkish craftsman, which Grandfather Gray had brought back from Constantinople. (I should say the memoirs had soon overflowed the writing case.)

Alex disliked her married name: too banal. Her father's polysyllabic 'Papapandelidis' inevitably became a boring joke. As her mother Aliki saw it. Aliki preferred her maiden name, 'Xenophon'. Alex could not very well avoid the Gray bit, but evolved the names under which she was registered in the books of the Nile Cold Storage at the Gare de Ramleh, Alexandria, and later, at David Jones, Sydney: Mme Alex Xenophon Demirjian Gray.

Alex acquired names as other women encrust themselves with jewels and bower-birds collect fragments of coloured glass. It mystified acquaintances that Mrs Gray should become, according to mood or period, 'Llewellyn' or 'Diacono' for instance, even briefly 'Bogdarly'. It was truly amazing that she should choose to be labelled 'Demirjian', when her mother-in-law, one of those she hated most, had been born a Demirjian (we think). The detested Magda could resign herself to 'Gray' from recognising in it a kind of inverted exoticism. So each of the women was more or less content, while inwardly despising contentment and each other.

I had known the Grays for years. We were all the incongruous descendants of Australian pastoral families. Henry was a cuckoo in the Gray nest, a scholar who wasted his years drifting through the Middle East collecting *objets d'art* and rare manuscripts. He brought them back to Sydney and founded an antique business which his son Hilary, my schoolfriend, developed profitably later on and the grandson Hal carried on somewhat fitfully.

Hilary, another of the Gray mavericks, was got on a Levantine woman, another *objet d'art* Henry brought back from Asia Minor before the war broke out between Turk and Greek and most of Smyrna was reduced to ash and rubble.

Henry's wife, Hilary's mother, was one of those women who acquire a reputation for beauty through a flair for clothes and jewels, an arresting body, and an aggressive kind of ugliness. She had her voice, too. She had her legs, and her taunting breasts. She stopped the conversation whenever she chose to appear at some Alexandrian *pâtisserie* during the six o'clock brouhaha. She would have stunned the Royal Sydney Golf Club if her breeding had allowed her access.

Most of the men who ran across her hoped they might take over from her husband, or her current lover. But although Magda Demirjian Gray took lovers, there was no indication that she would leave a husband, elderly certainly, but still virile, who kept her in style. In addition, their son Hilary, to whom she was not overly attached (Magda was attached only to herself) acted as a pledge between husband and wife that could not be overlooked.

Hilary had the appearance of a slender, green-complexioned Levantine rather than a rowdy extrovert Australian with pastoralist forebears. He had moist black eyelids and curving lashes. At school it got round that he was delicate and allowances must be made for this. He was given milk at break, and was allowed to sit in the sun reading books of his own choosing (Henry James and Proust) from under an eyeshade the colour of milk chocolate.

We saw a lot of each other as young boys. Hilary was welcome at our house, after school, and for week-ends. We cut up a frog in the bath to watch its heart movement, we smoked a cheroot under the buhl table in the hall, and we masturbated together in bed. We were quick to tidy up and it seemed to me at the time my parents were unaware of any of these activities. They must have been. For the friendship was brought to an abrupt end. It filtered back to me through maids' chatter and innuendo from the masters that my friend was an unhealthy influence: you couldn't expect much from the union of an Australian gentleman with an Armenian? Arab? Jewess? or whatever the woman was. So Hilary and I began to avoid each other at school. His mother had never been much more than a silhouette and a perfume. She did not fit into the acceptable, that is, dull Sydney society to which my parents belonged, but went down well with her husband's friends from the art-dealing and Bohemian worlds. (My mother heard that the Demijohn had done a belly dance on a dinner table at Vaucluse.)

Hilary and I were brought together again in the Second World War when we went over in uniform to the Middle East. There was no mention of the past, not even the flicker of an eyelash. I forget how Magda turned up in Cairo, but she did, announcing to an entourage of officers that she was there to do war work. Of what kind, nobody dared ask, and Magda merely slapped more orange powder on her cheeks and sucked on her lipstick. She became a reflection of those superb desert sunsets to the west of Mariut. Flaring her nostrils, lowering her eyelids, she suggested an inscrutable camel. But without becoming grotesque. She was a beauty by birth and of her milieu. Even Alex, who grew to hate her, had to admit it. As for Magda, she went her own way. She valued her independence and the respect of those she despised.

Hilary Gray was superficially wounded during the Syrian campaign. While on sick leave in Alexandria he met a girl, the daughter of Greeks from Asia Minor who had escaped to Egypt during the sack of Smyrna. I met the parents at the time Hilary was courting Alex. Once you got over the name 'Papapandelidis', they were very correct, even distinguished people, anglicised by governesses. They were distressed at the thought of their daughter marrying a man of whom nothing was known except that he came from a barbarous country, his father an antique dealer, his mother practically an untouchable from 'Frango Levantini' Smyrna.

I was with Stepho and Aliki Papapandelidis on the Alexandrian Corniche, across the bay the mole where the Pharos is believed to have stood.

'It is too soon, too soon,' Aliki was agonising.

'Too soon,' Stepho echoed in antiphon, his lips dragging on a frayed moustache.

Aliki was too proud to whimper. 'People lose their heads in revolutions and wars.'

'They are carried away into marriage and adultery.' A wind was ballooning Stepho's trousers.

'Half the children born in war or revolution are unwanted. Can you not do something, Lieutenant White, to help us?' She was looking at me hopefully, but without expectation.

'How can I alter the course of history?' It was what they knew.

'Exactly,' she said, and her husband echoed, 'Exactly.'

These decent people, in their dark clothes of another period, another fashion – I remember his anonymous tie, her carefully blacked lace-up shoes – were enacting a tragedy, nothing major, they themselves would have admitted, but a minor Alexandrian one, on the Corniche, across from the believed site of the Pharos.

They bowed their heads. Stepho was wearing a squashy Homburg, Aliki a black cloche.

The Papapandelides did not come to their daughter's wedding. Nor did Magda, perhaps out of discretion; she knew her place in Smyrna-Greek society.

Alex, at the time of her marriage, was a vision of camellia flesh asking to be bruised. Identical to Hilary's, her eyelids already showed signs of spoiling. Her pale, natural lips were parted, tremulous with the emotion waiting to spill out of them. Knowing Hilary, I could not believe she was still a virgin; it was the approaching sacrament which made her tremble and visualise a future breaking open in front of her.

The ceremony was performed by a Protestant padre. Some of Hilary's fellow officers and a batman were present. Myself the best man, on leave from my Air Force Wing at Sidi Haneish. As we came out of the church, two little Greek girls whose father kept a grocery on the corner flung handfuls of rice. It cut. I know because I experienced a few grains myself. It let loose some of the emotion Alex had bottled up. Her beautiful, pale, moist lips were overflowing with joy or grief. Hilary was trying to restrain his annoyance.

After a short honeymoon at Luxor Hilary returned to his regiment. When the Australians embarked for home and other theatres of war, he remained behind, attached to a British headquarters in the Western Desert. Alex returned to the parents' house at Schutz. There her children were born, first Hal, then towards the end of the war, Hilda.

Several times when on leave I was entertained to formal lunches by the Papapandelides. I found that Aliki's acquaintance addressed her as Madame Xenophon and that Madame X's husband was wedded to the telephone. He was always waiting to be called to it. He would jump up, dropping his napkin and his cutlery to accept an invitation to *le bridge* and *le thé*. In fact most of this Smyrna gentleman's life had been spent at bridge and tea, or in writing complimentary verses to the ladies of his circle. When he died of a stroke in the garden at Schutz near the end of the war, the ladies sighed, as they wiped the porto from their lips before the next rubber. '*Ce pauvre Stepho Pa-pa-pan, il était si gentil . . .*' and soon forgot.

Once in the garden at Schutz after lunch the pretty dolls of children tumbling round our ankles, their mother in a flowing tussore dress, I asked Alex, 'Do they see much of their other granny?' (for Magda was still around, between Cairo and Alexandria). Alex raised her upper lip with its steely pinpricks of afternoon perspiration and replied, 'I'll leave Mamma to answer that one.'

When asked, Aliki pursed her mouth and faintly smiled; she had complained earlier that she was starting a migraine. 'In Smyrna we met, I think once or twice. We didn't know them.' The faint smile dissolved in a silvery mist of painful recollection.

Aliki could dare anyone to disagree with her standards. In appearance she was to Magda what an etching is to a painting. Aliki's lines had been scratched remorselessly into the copper. Magda was a series of flat, splattered planes reflecting whichever continent or island she happened to inhabit at the moment it was done. Aliki was Greek: she had suffered wars, invasions, revolutions; Magda the Levantine had battened on these, along with the black marketeers and the lovers an occupation throws up.

In later life Aliki visited her grandchildren in Australia, but could not be persuaded by their mother to stay. She missed the scents of thyme and stocks, and the smell of burnt-out candles. 'Though I am not a believer,' Aliki assured us, 'the smell of an Orthodox church is consoling.'

The last time I saw Magda she was down on her luck. It was on a balcony in the Delta town of Mansoura. I had been sent to Egypt by Alex to order the Government to surrender property they had confiscated when foreigners were expelled. Of course they refused, but I had my meeting with Magda. The henna of her hair and the orange powder with which her cheeks were ingrained outdid the Nile sunset. 'Keeping old age at bay,' she explained when she caught me looking too closely at her. Her laughter reeked of cheap Egyptian cigarettes. From inside the block came the smell of burning cottonseed and someone was cooking a pot of beans. 'No,' she said, 'you won't see me again. Oh, no, no! What should I do in Australia but die?' Nor did we see her. Not long after my visit, the building in which she was living collapsed, as buildings in provincial Egypt will.

Aliki Xenophon settled in mainland Greece when the Second World War was over. I met her there in Athens, and on the island of Nisos. The old cardigans she wore, in black or sepia wool, were as ravelled as post-war Greece. In her character she remained as severe as ever. As an old woman the *archontissa* was writing something on Bouboulina, the pirate queen who led the war in the Aegean against the Turk which resulted in her country's independence.

Independence: the grand illusion to which a trio of incongruously related women – Aliki, Magda, and Alex – were unswervingly dedicated. From which of these women Hilda's character derived, I sometimes wondered.

At first appearance, her mother's slave, she was also her mother's keeper: she kept the archives, as opposed to Alex's arcane memoirs. Whether archives or memoirs contained the truth it might be difficult to decide. Fossicking through the memoirs was not a job I looked forward to, but I had a sense of duty to this family whose lives were intertwined with mine. The expression of Hilda's face when she made the proposition dared me to reject it. Although an Anglo-Saxon Australian on both sides, I am a sybarite and masochist; some of the dramatis personae of this Levantine script could be the offspring of my own psyche.

So, I submitted, with misgivings.

Notes
p. 14   Schutz: suburb of Alexandria
p. 16   *archontissa*: Greek noblewoman

Memoirs of Alex Xenophon Demirjian Gray

I don't know where to begin what may turn out a monstrous mistake – start at the beginning? Plunge in today? Who knows where the end will come – and whether in a flash, or a long gnawing. In any case THEY will be watching, from inside the house, from the garden, the Park, or most disturbingly, from above.

I have been feeling sick this morning. I don't think I have started a terminal illness. Or have I? Anyhow, foreboding has got me down. And Tipsy has just vomited a half-digested bird.

I am lying on the daybed in a strip of sunlight in Hilary's study. 'Where is Daddy?' I call to Hilda.

'But he isn't *here*.'

Wonder why I christened her Hilda? Should it have been Hulda? What I needed was a saint, and what I got was a ferret.

Oh, God! Oh, my little Panayia! Mamma, where are you?

Hilda was already on her way from the kitchen with my morning marrow-on-toast and lemon-barley water. Our daughter is a good soul, but dull. Her face is furrowed with that earnestness which turns it grey by the brightest light. She will never find a man to accept that grey earnestness.

'Don't tell me your father went in to buy his cheroots without asking if there was anything I needed.'

She stood the tray with the toast and barley water on the lacquer table beside the daybed. (I sensed she was trying to have a discreet look at my manuscript.)

'But what is it you need, Mother?'

'What I need?'

She was looking greyer than ever. She must have inherited it from *his* side, a true Gray (a horrid pun I realise every time I come up with it, but unavoidable).

'I could have thought of *something* – if only a button – to show I play a part in his life.'

'Eat your toast, Mother. It's so nourishing.'

'How you bully me, darling! Everybody does – your father ... And can't you scoop up Tipsy's vomit and throw it into the hydrangeas?'

'Not Tipsy, Mother. It's Trifle.'

'Where is Tipsy?'

'Tipsy's dead.'

If true, it makes me so unhappy. I still see my old Tipsy, trailing her tail, her blue form traipsing, limping across the terrace, it is the hip with the pin. Once the fur had grown nobody noticed the cheek an earlier car had smashed. All these wounds inflicted on what one holds dearest ...

Now I can't prevent myself crying. 'You're trying to remind me that Hilary – my husband – your father – is dead.'

Hilda goes away, screwing up her face. In the end, like all helpful people, she is no help. Nobody understands one but oneself.

Though they like to suggest I am deaf, I can hear her making a call in the kitchen.

'Hal? She's worse this morning. What are we going to do? ... Oh, no, Dr Parslow's a nice man, but have you any faith? ... *Not* Falkenberg! She'll never accept Falkenberg ...'

For once in her life Hilda is right.

From the moment he held my hand I realised he was a dangerous man. Cold skin, steely eyes and hair, a hawk's beak. '... a brilliant woman, then why do you choose to behave like a little girl?' I avoid looking at him. 'Did your father make you sleep with him?' 'My father was a silly man, his pathetic little verses completely lacking in style. How could I sleep with "Pa-pa-pan"?' Hoping to impress me my mentor quoted in a throbbing voice from *The Tragedy of Man* (translating from the Hungarian) and some of the more odious platitudes of Goethe. He wanted me to sleep with him. Well, I did – once or twice. It was as if knives were entering my womb. But I laughed at him – too hysterically perhaps? From there on he threatened me. Because I was not sufficiently impressed by his performance he had me locked up.

From the kitchen, 'Are you coming over, Hal? Or are you going to leave me to deal with it?' Hilda on the verge of blubbering.

I have never expected much of our children, nor they of each other. I have never expected anything of anyone, except myself – and cats.

Blubbery Hilda: 'The only ones who ever managed to manage Mother were the grandmothers.'

Which? Magda the Monster? Or my darling Mouse?

Magda! In Port Said they called her French. Probably Syro-Maltese-Jewish. I never saw her father, but *know* him. A squat, hairy male armed with whistle and flag on the platform at Benha, where he was station master.

And the masterful Magda became an Australian lady. If

she slapped the face of a disobedient Australian nanny, nobody dared question the justice of her act, least of all the nanny herself. To democratic eyes she was superb. No wonder she seduced Henry, the authority on Byzantine history and Middle Eastern artefacts, or that he died of her.

I can't remember when Magda died (no doubt Hilda can, but I shan't ask her). I thought I was going to die after changing trains at Benha, and daring to eat a pickled herring on the gritty platform, where another squat, hairy man with whistle and flag had replaced Magda's Syro-Maltese – or Armenian-Jewish station master father.

As I was flung about by diarrhoea in a primitive 'French' Port Said hotel, I marvelled at Magda's constitution and her commitment to survival.

Hilda has returned from the telephone.

'Isn't Hal coming over, darling?'

Hilda: 'No.'

'I knew he wouldn't. It's possibly better for all of us.'

Hilda only answers obliquely. 'Hal has his own affairs.'

'I realised that long ago. The priest – the New York Jewish convert to Catholicism – such a handsome man – it was easy enough to understand – and difficult not to resent Hal's good taste and good fortune. In fact, it's more or less the reason I haven't wanted your brother around.'

Hilda contains her feelings.

'And you, Hilda – what about *your* affairs?'

'You've never left me scope for them, Mother.'

'Would you, I wonder – would either of you have married – if Hilary and I hadn't been your parents?'

'Oh, let's leave the subject – Mummy!'

'I would have been better as a father, and often was.'

'You haven't finished your marrow toast.'

'No. It's nasty this morning. It smells of fish. I could have vomited it up like Tipsy – no, Trifle's bird.'

'Trifle's mess looks ghastly, I admit. I must scrape it up, and throw it under the hydrangeas.'

'Marrow isn't what Magda prescribed. Snipe shit on buttered toast is what she and her aunt loved for their elevenses – her Diacono aunt.'

'I never heard about the aunt.'

'She brought her to Egypt after the Catastrophe.'

'I never heard.'

'You must have been told. But none of the Grays had memories.'

'Not for what is disgusting. I don't remember the snipe. And I can't bear "words".'

'Shit is real, isn't it? You've always been on about what is real. Those silly old papers of yours – the so-called archives.'

'The record of our preposterous lives.'

'Archives are only half the truth. That's why I'm writing my memoirs. Archives have no soul. You wouldn't understand that. Or why snipe shit isn't necessarily putrescence. On days when there weren't any snipe, Magda and the aunt would be tucking into gulls' eggs or sea urchins on the terrace.'

'What was the aunt's name?'

'Magda.'

'*Another* Magda.'

'Isn't that what I said?'

She is shuffling the things on the tray. 'I'm going to ring Professor Falkenberg, Mother.'

'You're not! You're not, Hilda!'

'You must see *somebody*. You need treatment. It's too great a responsibility. I haven't a trained mind.'

'A trained mind? That's where you give yourself away as an Australian. You resent my not having sent you to the Uni. Poor little you.'

I might have pulled her leg some more if the situation hadn't become so serious. Falkenberg's constraining hands – those knobbly joints and little tufts of dark hair . . .

She continues walking towards the kitchen as I call after her, 'Hilda, I promise to be good if you promise not to ring him. I couldn't bear to be locked up – *again* – with a lot of mad geriatrics farting at me for the rest of my life – telling me about the jewellery and furniture their daughters-in-law have stolen from them – their husbands' prostates – their grandchildren . . . Hilda?'

She marches on. She slams the kitchen door.

I grow more and more desperate. Forgetting my arthritic hip, and that Trifle is stretched alongside the daybed, I jump up. I almost trip on Hilary's favourite Bokhara.

She is scraping plates, making room amongst other odds and ends of washing up.

'You wouldn't be so cruel, would you? I couldn't bear those mad old women and their grandchildren.'

Her lips are stitched tight together.

'At least I haven't got grandchildren. Unless you're hiding something from me. Not you, but Hal. Perhaps Hal has a child by his Jewish priest.'

She is staring out of the window. The yard has never looked so bland, so deceitful, the lavender bush alight with bees, doves balancing on the tightrope of a power line. Can I believe that Hilda is about to relent?

'I'll ring Patrick then – you like him – and ask him to advise us what to do.'

I like Patrick, as much as you can like anyone who is against you.

'I liked him well enough till I sent him to Egypt to persuade the Government to return the property which is mine by rights. He got together with Magda instead and she persuaded him to let her keep it.'

'Magda died when the building collapsed.'

'I wonder. Even if she did it doesn't mean she didn't have the property put in her name. It doesn't mean that Patrick and Magda – you too, perhaps, didn't concoct something to your advantage.'

'Very well. If that's what you believe.'

She has begun filling the sink. After Hilda finishes washing up, she always flings the water off the rubber gloves, and it hisses as it hits the dregs of detergent. I do not want to hear this.

'Right, Hilda. I agree, I'll do all the washing up – if I can drag the rings off my fingers. I'll see and talk to Patrick. He's nice.' (I can feel my teeth gnashing.) 'We'll have a good old *pow-wow*. If only you'll believe in me – both of you.'

Did I I I believe in what I was saying? Hilary was Patrick's friend, they cut up frogs together in the bath, they . . .

He was our best MAN.

There is no reason why I shouldn't like – love the old sod. (Bet he blues his hair.)

When it's a question of saving myself, I'll unpack my uniform, the tarnished 'pips' – isn't it what they were called? the service ribbons – the food spots which declare themselves most volubly on old musty drill which has not completely lost the smell of male armpits. Patrick will appreciate all of that.

Hilda does not answer. She has started the washing up

I have promised to do. She knows me, not the essential part, but she knows – the worst.

Too much truth exhausts. 'I am going up to rest, darling. You can ring Patrick and tell me what you've arranged between you.'

I pick up Trifle to take her upstairs. There's nothing like a cat in bed – a trustworthy hot-water bottle. When she scratched my cleavage, naturally I threw her down. She yowled as she hit the skirting-board. So in the end you can't trust anybody, not even a cat.

My little daughter smiles sourly, as though knowing it all from the very beginning. Hilda won't forgive; cats do, through indifference to fate.

Upstairs I sink down on the bed, on the Arachova blanket Aliki sent to remind us of other times. I listen to the pricking of insects like the stitching of peasant blankets, warm cold pine-needles, and the rustle of birds as they revolve with the terracotta seed-dish suspended from a bough of the eucalypt closest to the window.

I am dreaming, I suppose. After we escaped from Smyrna, there was very little to keep us warm, unless each other. Mamma drew me down beside her under the Turkish rug Mrs Bogdarly had given us out of charity. All else burnt in the fire which swept us towards the Quay. The buttons of the officer carrying me ground into my cheeks. The French were kind but their teeth expected reparation. I was glad to be returned to Mamma, to huddle with her on the deck of the destroyer, along with our basket, and Smaragda, her kerchief smelling of smoke and its last laundering on Asian soil.

Uncles and cousins came to look at us in Egypt. They lent us the empty house at Schutz. Mamma said furniture

was unimportant if we had our lives. Smaragda seemed to
have disappeared with her sweetly laundered kerchief. She
was, it appeared, preparing to die anyway. So Mamma and
I huddled together for company and warmth under Mrs
Bogdarly's Turkish rug. Mamma said the Jews had been
through it already also the Armenians now it is the Greeks'
turn not the rich ones the uncles and cousins whose furniture we might damage. We might have frozen if it hadn't
been for Mrs Bogdarly, who gave us in addition to the rug
the little table with the brazier underneath so that we were
able to sit on the floor our feet stretched out towards the
coals and warmth. I missed our dear Smaragda Papa I don't
remember much he had been taken up said Mamma by
some of his Samos relatives and the Alexandrian bridge-
players.

I hear the gate. I hear the doorbell bruising my sleep
then Hilda opening the front door. It will be Patrick coming
as promised. You can rely on Patrick even when you don't
much want him. It was Hilda's idea, better anyway than
Falkenberg and the straitjacket he might prescribe, I can get
round Patrick.

I must allow Hilda time to give the real account of her
troubles to her confidant. I must make the most of my
beauty. I love the smell of make-up. People have often
told me I am an actress by instinct, not realising I am that
by profession. Sometimes I surprise strangers, even relatives, by performing my monologues *Dolly Formosa and the
Happy Few*. Patrick is less surprised than others because he
too is a performer. Yes, I am less inclined to expose myself
to Patrick. Hilary used to say Patrick and I have the same
eyes. My eyes have always taken strangers by surprise. The
ignorant don't expect a blue-eyed Greek.

Some old woman who thought she knew me, some Gray cousin, told me years ago, 'You are your own worst enemy.' I told her back, 'And you are a boring, meddling, self-satisfied, Australian Protestant bitch.' Of course she hated me ever after. People don't dare to be told the truth about themselves.

On the afternoon of Patrick's visit, all hibiscus trumpets and gold spangles, I decide to wear a sari I had bought – Delhi? Lahore? No, it was given me by the man whose BO was scented over with sandalwood. One of Magda's lovers, her Gazelle she called him. She could never forgive me the sari she considered hers by rights. Poor Magda was a silly old cunt. It infuriated Hilary when I called his mother a cunt, but how could I help it when her cunt was the most functional part of her body – and her mind. It had also brought forth her son, who was one of my major disasters.

Lovers who marry young are often quickly turned into an indeterminate sex where they remain until it is decided who is husband, who wife. The afternoon of Patrick's visit the glass shows me up. In spite of the lovely film of sari, the pale lipstick, the black liner framing the shameful un-Greek blue of my eyes, I can see the grains of powder trembling on the hairs of the moustache, feel the more-than-down on my forearms, details of the disguise Hilary had forced on me as part of a pre-meditated revenge.

It was like that the day we caught up with each other in a back room of the seamy Macleay Street hotel. (It was registered as 'private'.) Actually it was Patrick who had run Hilary to earth, then left us to work out what we expected of each other. I could feel my moustache trembling with rage, Hilary sitting smooth and silky in front of an exercise book. 'What do you think you are doing?' I asked. 'Writing my memoirs.' 'Was there any need to walk out on us to do it?' 'I couldn't stand any more of that barrack of a house.' 'When I made the house so nice for you.' 'You made the *house* ...? A stage for your performances!'

Hilda starts calling from the foot of the stairs, 'Aren't you coming down, Mother?'

'I was lying down – dozing. I thought you'd come up and wake me when I was wanted.'

'But you've been awake for ages. We could hear you moving about.'

You can't put anything across little Hilda.

'I had to get dressed, hadn't I? And give you and Patrick time to share your secrets. I'm sure there are plenty of those.'

'Oh, don't be paranoid, darling!'

I can't postpone it any longer. One last look at myself in the glass. I am Alex once more. Even Hilary would approve if he were to come in through the glass doors, into the living room, and throw down his hat like the man I had always been looking for, untainted by Papa's bridge game, or the *mœurs* of Magda's male seraglio. I am so excited I trip on the lowest stair and am propelled through the hall into the living room.

Hilda and Patrick look so shocked I might have been drinking.

'What do you think ... of doing?' Hilda mumbles over her thinned-out lips.

'I thought of asking Patrick to take me into the Park this divine day ...'

Patrick is looking his primmest in a buttoned-up raincoat.

Though he has been in the house some time he has not thought of parking his umbrella.

Hilda says, 'You'd better put on a coat at least.'

I could have cried. 'But I want to share my sari with people. All those poor wretches who escape to the Park from their slums.' I burble, when normally it is my daughter who blubbers. 'You always *crab* me!'

Patrick tries to mend the situation. 'There's no need, darl, to come unstuck. We all love you.'

Hilda has gone out of the room, she returns with a coat. 'You'll have to wear something, Mother, on a day like this.'

She hands the coat to Patrick, who begins to get me into it. Hilda could never bear to touch me. (I've changed your sheets too often – as though I could help it.) If I had been Danny – she groomed his coat, bathed his eyes, massaged his legs after he developed arthritis. A dog was a different matter. If ever I ask my daughter to rub my chest or back, I encounter, not a soft daughterly hand, but a hard little wincing knuckle or fist.

Patrick is doing up the tarnished buttons of what was Hilary's army great-coat. H. had kept it as a nostalgic gesture to the masochistic self I so despised. For me the coat still had in it the sand H. brought back when on leave from the Western Desert, and the stiffness of glassy, desert winters. He would throw it off, strip entirely, before we fell on the bed to perform the acts of what we both believed to be love.

I hate those buttons. I still bear scars from the first (clothed) embrace of the returning soldier.

Patrick murmurs, 'There!' and pats my stomach with what he understands as tenderness.

'Have a good walk.' Hilda throws open the door to bring me down to what she understands as earth.

She may have been right. The hibiscus has shed its spangles, the trumpets are wilted phalluses.

I hear myself whimpering as we wind down the pebbled path. Patrick restrains me whenever I threaten to fall.

'Nobody understands what I am.'

'Oh, come on, you're too full of self-pity, Alex.'

'They don't – or do – but don't. They don't understand that I'm frail. My husband doesn't – my children – you, Patrick. Perhaps only my Mamma – the Bouboulina who gave in to her weak daughter when she mistook lust for love, but understood too well my struggle to create two little resistant babies. Oh, hell, yes!'

We stumble on, silent, against rain and wind.

The Park is empty. None of the characters with whom I would have shared my lovely sari. I would have danced for them to sitar and cymbal. I would have offered them that part of myself which is full of joy in life. Not the gross grey swollen travesty of a human being who in the present circumstances fills the whole park, trampling in dog-shit, trailing the hem of Hilary's coat in mud.

'Far too many dogs, Patrick.'

'Too many people in need of consolation.'

He can be an old bore.

'Oh yes! We know *that*! That's why Hilary got himself Danny. He imagined he needed consolation for our marriage. He became involved with a cocker spaniel – the maddest of all breeds. I wonder whether he saw it as the alter ego of his wife. Could have been. He got himself a male cocker.'

The weather is growing dirtier. Near the stone bridge,

Patrick has to help me through the bog which develops during excessive rain. In the branches of the twisted willow, which Jews from the Junction tear to pieces at Succoth to build their tabernacles on identical unit balconies, perches a family of dejected mynas. They should have been humming birds. I almost abandon the army coat to induce humming birds to appear. I would have danced, though clogged with mud to the ankles.

Instead, Patrick drags me across the bridge. I think I heard him mutter, 'You asked for it, didn't you!' Perhaps our friendship lasts because he recognises a fellow masochist, and here we are linked in this desolate park, where the clouds might still split open on patches of Tiepolo blue, but don't.

It is not one of those days. It is a day for memories bogged down in mud and recrimination.

'Let's get home as quickly as possible,' I beg, 'to a cup of tea.'

'You wanted to come.'

'Have you, of all people, never found you were wrong?'

He doesn't answer, but drags me on through increasing bog. Dark threads of blood dangle from the nostrils of the ficus, the hairs from its armpits sway in the wind.

We plod.

And arrive.

Hilda sits us down to strong Indian tea (always gives me indigestion) and crumpets oozing butter from every pore. But first she rids me of my muddy shoes. She has brought a chipped enamel basin from which Danny used to drink. She bathes my feet, my ankles in particular. Is Hilda after all a saint in disguise?

Some of the crumpet butter drips into the basin. It spreads like gold coins on the surface of the water.

Hilda my daughter is really the nanny my mother didn't engage for me, and Patrick, a little unwanted brother.

I cannot prevent myself weeping. The tears spread amongst the gold coins in Danny's enamel drinking basin.

Hilda asks, 'Why cry when it's what you wanted and did – wasn't it!'

'Yes, I know. I shot Danny.'

'You did it of your own free will.'

I bowed my head to my knees. 'He was old, and smelly. Everyone old and smelly deserves . . .'

'Do they, though?'

An unfair thrust.

I try to conjure up the picture of myself in earlier days walking Danny through the Park's pine plantation, snuffing up the scent of needles and resin, waiting for him to lift a leg. Instead I can only see him lying, tongue protruding, chin flattened on the concrete floor, eyes like rotten periwinkles rimmed with scarlet.

'Hilary never forgave me. Bad enough to banish his smelly old dog to the coal bunker. I mean, you couldn't have had him in the house. I mean, could you?'

They are both silent in the presence of my evocation.

Then Patrick says, 'He forgave to some extent. Hilary came back, didn't he? To live with his family. He understood that smells are inevitable.'

'He came back. Oh God, YES!'

Hilda grabs the basin, slopping some of the water on the moth-eaten Afghan rug. She carries the basin away, always slopping, over the Bokhara, the Baluch. Her shoulders express all.

'Yes,' I am shouting. 'No need to tell me. But you'll both accuse me for ever. When it was I who bore the worst of it. It was I who found him hanging by the cord in the coal bunker where his dog had lived out the last of his life. Hilary – so beautiful in the beginning – as you, Patrick, know.'

It is darkening outside amongst the hibiscus and the eucalypts.

'So now, leave me, both of you.'

'I don't know what you are talking about.'

It is Hilda speaking on her return.

But Patrick goes.

I am possessed by this doomed wish to telephone somebody who will understand, not Mamma, that would be too much to hope, Nadya Bogdarly – perhaps, who gave us the rug which kept us warm as refugees, and the table with the brazier underneath, towards which we stretched our toes during those Alexandrian winters.

There was a wall telephone at the Bogdarlys. In moments of crisis one almost wrung the handle off. Many the *cris de cœur* Nadya's telephone listened to, as well as love whispers, and some raspberries.

During the war, Hilary away in the W.D., I would lunch at Nadya's every other day. She kept open house for her less affluent or less generous relatives, those vast sisters, and British staff officers who had got through their allowances too quickly. Élie Bogdarly was senile by then. Nadya, who started vast like the sisters, had shrunk. Her face was mapped with the rivers of Mesopotamia, Tigris and Euphrates, picked out, it seemed, in their actual silt (Nadya suffered from blackheads).

The day I remember in particular nobody had favoured Nadya's table except one of its most regular patrons, Colonel Cyril Ogdon-Bloodworth. Nadya's unreliable bladder had forced her to leave the room for a moment. Élie was banging on the table with his spoon. I tried to quieten him, 'Don't worry, Élie. Your mummy will be back to give you your second helping.' Mohammed the saffragi, nobody, would have dared help the master of the house to his moussaka in his wife's absence. The Colonel sat drumming on the table, eyeing the enormous dish of moussaka, probably wondering whether he could put away a second helping before tucking into the *riz à l'Impératrice* which invariably followed at the Bogdarlys.

Élie hammered and hammered with his spoon, on his face the persecuted expression of the senile.

After wresting his stomach into a fresh position the Colonel broke into a confidential mutter, 'Last night in a taxi between the Union and the Cecil, a girl – or perhaps it was a woman – the light could have been flattering to her – this person Magda Demisomething actually sucked me off. Most extraordinary – or wasn't it? Wouldn't know this Magda, would you?'

'I ought to.'

'What a war brings out in people!' He heaved and rumbled and broke into the giggles. 'Shocking isn't it?'

At this point Nadya returned. 'Terrible, yes, we have all been through it – several in a lifetime.'

By now I had caught the Colonel's giggles. The image of my mother-in-law and Colonel Bloodworth's shuddering thighs in the musty confines of an Egyptian taxi was more than I could take.

'Quiet, Daddy! Mummy will give you your second helping.' The map of Nadya's face, the whole Mesopotamian basin, had broken up for the tragedy of war, the tragedy of life and her husband-child. 'Terrible, terrible!' she moaned.

The Colonel rocked, racked by his giggles, and I more disgracefully by mine.

Colonel Ogdon-Bloodworth's hard war ended by his falling off a roof at Mazarita after a surfeit of pigeons and rice and several litres of rough red, followed by chasers of Bolonaki whisky from a Johnny Walker bottle.

The Park is no longer visible. I am left stranded in this darkened room during one of the intervals in my life's play.

'What is it, Mother?' Hilda asks.

'Nothing – everything. The Bogdarlys in particular, Nadya was my friend. Colonel What's-It could I suppose, be one of the many roles one plays.'

'I think you'd better go to bed and sleep it off.'

'Oh, but you know I never sleep – or no, you wouldn't. I only dream.'

Her hard, matter-of-fact body refuses to accept the truth. It shores me up as we mount the stairs, up, up, to another stage of purgatory.

I lie there for hours, years, as I knew I would, turning and turning. Remembering scenes from the past. The room fills with branches of smoke, concealing none of us from the flames, the figures, which have burst out all along the Prokymaia. If I could touch our old Smaragda's crumpled face it might act as a talisman, when the uproar died I could hear the voice at least amongst the furniture of this nightbound room.

'Lord save thy people and bless their inheritance. Lord save ... and ... bless ...'

Old voices, ancient words – the prayers of those who, like Smaragda, are scarcely in need of them. Their own goodness is their salvation. Who, of all these peasant women, trailing from shrine to shrine, worshipping the worm-eaten faces of Panayia and saints, in a golden haze of candlelight, could have played as I had, the role of Magda Demirjian crouched between Cyril Bloodworth's shuddering thighs? But do I *want* absolution from the sins I have committed – perpetuated? That is a difficult one to answer.

'What is it?' Hilda's voice from across the landing.

'Nothing.'

'You sounded as though you were being murdered.'

'I was praying.'

She appears by my bed holding a torch. She had plaited her hair for the night. The plaits hang either side of her face in two little nondescript rats' tails.

'Oh well,' she says, 'that's something I would *not* understand. I'm a rationalist, as you know.'

'You're entitled, darling, to your own form of mumbo-jumbo.'

'Then you admit ...?'

'Oh, I don't *know*! Leave me. However they torment me I must find out whether the lives I have lived amount to anything. I have always been searching, however squalid the circumstances, Onouphrios, for instance ...'

'Onouphrios?'

'He was the monk at Ayia Ekaterini. However he disgusted me, I liked to think that by serving him patiently it was a kind of penance which might in time lead to salvation. I wore the habit. I was Cassianí in those days.'

'Try to sleep. Shall I bring you a cup of warm milk with some honey in it?'

'No. You must have been reading the Cartland woman. I'll try to think of my friend Bernadette. A dear soul. I was Benedict then.'

'Aren't you getting your Churches mixed?'

'Oh, I've had my Roman interlude too. I've had to try everything.'

Her torch fades.

'Everything. Do you hear? Of course you don't want to listen to reason. Hilda Gray – a nail in one's coffin.'

We meet next morning in the kitchen. I have got there before her.

'I feel so refreshed.' I could tell my cheeks were glowing like one of those apples in an expensive fruit shop.

'Then you must have slept in spite of your determination not to.'

'I must have. Yes, I did. I meditated on the Dormition, until I was uplifted.'

I had fixed myself a pot of porridge. Seeing it, Hilda made herself as narrow as possible before indulging in her tea and toast.

She has lowered her eyes. Is porridge dribbling down my chin? I try to explore with my tongue, to suck the stuff back, to avoid causing Hilda further distress.

I tell her – only on the spur of the moment, 'I'm going into the city this morning – to do the shops, to see my lawyers, to . . .'

'Do you think you're up to it?'

The lawyers must have frightened her.

'Why not? I've never felt healthier.'

She stands scuffling the crockery in the sink.

I set out. She watches me leave. Hilda would like to think she is my banker, but I have a little money put away, and take some of this in a chamois bag round my neck, under my simple frock – grey for a pilgrimage.

I swing along. On the bus everybody is looking at me.

As I am a great observer of people we meet half-way. I smile at them, some, if not all, smile back. The disbelievers make me wonder whether my face looks naked because of its natural glow of health. I decide my first port of call must be a store where I can buy myself a lipstick.

The great store is humming with activity. Even with so many people to distract attention from eccentricity, it would have embarrassed me to dive down inside my dress and wrest a note from the chamois leather bag. Far simpler to help oneself to a lipstick in passing: so many of them, and practically unattended by the languid girls made up to promote their wares. No one is interested in my performance. I pass on with the lipstick in my hand and head for what is called the LADIES.

Nobody inside. I can let my imagination loose. I begin to sing, *I shook the flowering almond tree* ... in honour of my Greek origins and attack my mouth with the new lipstick. It is of the bloodiest tone, far up the scale from the almond blossom of the song. Not incongruous really, when you think that blood may run from any Greek at any moment. As I smooth my parted lips against each other with the expertise of the professional actress, I notice written on the white tiles beside the glass, *let a woman tell you most women are cunts*, I prickle at first, then write underneath it, *let another woman add, the same hole can be found in the majority of men*. I twirl. I feel so free. I have a great desire to dance. Anyone who witnessed my performance at the charity ball in the Adolf Hitler Hotel, Washington DC, in whatever the year, will know that I am no mean danseuse. A few more twirls and I dash off another piece of advice in lippie on the virgin wall opposite, *If men are pricks don't lie down miz grow a prick of your own.*

After this I return to the busy world of the store proper. The door of the LADIES gasps as I leave, the glass of the outside world dazzles, the escalators threaten to throw me.

I must have been more noticeable than before thanks to my lipstuck mouth. It was to some extent unfortunate because I had to accomplish another mission: something in which to carry my newly acquired lippie. In the circumstances I could only snatch clumsily in passing, and my hand came away with a glaring patent-leather handbag (not at all my style).

After drawing breath I opened it and put my lipstick inside. Then as I snapped the clasp shut I heard the voice, 'That's the one. A real professional.' It was a hard-faced female, corseted inside regulation black, on top of all, a black parting through yellow hair.

A male grabbed me by the elbow.

At the police station my instincts prompted me to try a cry: no woman will throw away recklessly the traditional advantages her sex gives, '... but I can pay for the things – I promise!' I moaned, as I rummaged in my breasts for the chamois leather bag.

'You oughter know better at your age. And what's yer family up to – letting you out? No sense of responsibility towards their granny.'

'Officer, please! You don't know what you're doing to me. No one is old. It's only their bodies. And then not always. My body has never let me down.'

This great, blue-eyed, moustachioed booby turned aside as though he had been offered a basinful of sick. I saw that eyelashes, tears, would not help in my defence.

'What's your number?' he asked.

'My number? Am I a prisoner? Or a hospital case?'

'Yer family must have a telephone number.'

'I was never any good at figures.'

'You must know your own name, don't yer?'

'Dolor.'

'But yer family name – and where you live.'

'My family name is Gray, and we are scattered throughout the world.'

The Great Booby cannot restrain a belch.

He disappeared behind the scenes, where I could hear him, 'A real nut. Says 'er name is Gray. Pages of 'em in the book. Any'ow, the old bitch doesn't want to remember the number.'

At the same instant I saw my chance. I floated free, outside the police station, down a lane, up another, corners away I was relieved to find I had escaped the Law.

I began walking seriously. I walked and walked. My lipstuck mouth worried me a lot. I shot inside the great cathedral opposite and scrubbed myself with holy water from the stoup, not without twinges for what I might be contracting from so much holy slime (my daughter's face appeared to me). I dried myself on a pamphlet advertising a retreat, then I sat for a moment to give thanks to Whomsoever it is in this gloomy Irish sanctuary. From the glances of various custodians I realised the Holy Spirit would have wished me to move on.

Again I flitted. I walked and walked. My feet were hurting dreadfully. From time to time I rested on benches. Sliding my hand between the slats of one of these, I realised my foot might have got caught between them if I had been a little girl, and there I might have stuck till the paddy-wagon arrived. So I limped on hurriedly. Better septic blisters than the Great Booby with the tartar moustache and the belly swelling over his belt.

Oh dear, if only it were possible to pause indefinitely to absorb the beauty of life instead of escape from its ugliness. But necessity drove me on. I began to worry too, about my manuscript, locked in its case, and in one of its many hiding places. Hilda might organise a search, call in Patrick, even Hal and his friend the priest the Jewish convert to Catholicism. Their treachery apart, my hand itched to record the events of a memorable day. I tried to console myself with the knowledge that my memory never lets me down. Even so my right hand twitched as I ticked off the names of the bays I passed: Rushcutters, Double, Rose, Parsley (wasn't it Parsley where I lost my bra on a moonlight night to an American?) and ever onward.

That evening I might have ended in the sea if I hadn't been led to a little white weatherboard cottage looking out over an inlet. An elderly couple seated on a homemade wooden bench, surrounded by a forest of giant dahlias, could have been admiring the sunset. I knew at once this was my destination, there was such inherent goodness in these old people, they could only welcome me as parents welcome a long lost child.

However, a prodigal never has it all that easy. I began to babble, 'Do you realise this is almost exactly like Abukir? The houses are in the same style.'

The woman made a sound like a goose's warning.

'Or Cranz. The Russians used to go to Cranz before the Revolution. The wealthy ones of course. There's amber buried in the sand dunes. The Germans still find amber in them.'

It was the man this time who cleared his throat at the mention of Russians and Germans.

I must say something to convince these 'parents' I am worthy of a welcome.

'Do you know that you can tell genuine amber from false by rubbing it on tissue paper. If the paper sticks ...'

The sunset was waning. Tardy gulls in the foreground sailed against an opalescence.

In desperation I said to the female parent, 'May I rest a little? I've walked so far.'

Without giving permission, she moved closer to her husband, making room on her side.

I was so grateful. I must have sounded as desperate as I felt, for the man unstuck his lips.

'Out late, aren't yer? An elderly person might run inter trouble.'

'That might happen at any time of day.'

'That's correct,' the man agreed, and the woman said, 'Terrible what happens to people. Your family will be worrying.'

'I don't think so.'

They were shocked into silence for a while.

'There must be someone we can notify,' the man said at last.

'We haven't the phone. He could walk up to the public box, but it's a stiff pull and he's got the emphysema.'

'I don't want to put anybody out.'

The silence became more tormented.

The man broke it, 'Any'ow, I'm Frank Dobbin – retired from the ferries. And this is Mollie, a assistant manageress at Kurrajong Heights in the old days.'

They waited for me to label myself.

I rooted around. 'I'm Eleanor Shadbolt. I've done almost everything in my day.'

They laughed to cover their disbelief.

I would have liked to sit and just breathe beside them, unmolested. Insects were at work inside the great satiny cushions of the dahlias, their droppings landed in my salt cellars. A spider descended on a thread.

'Had your tea?' the woman asked.

'I can't remember. I don't think so. No.' I tried not to shock them unduly.

'It's late for most people. But we haven't neether,' said Frank. 'We suit ourselves.'

He sounded proud. It was their contribution to unconventional living.

They must have accepted I should share their lives for the time being. All three of us rose from the bench and went inside. Their interior was as scrubbed and shipshape as you would have expected. Soon there was steak spitting in the pan and water boiling for the eggs waiting at room temperature. The steak was for the man, eggs with dripping veils draped over watery toast for the women.

My eyes clouded, then blurred with gratitude as we ate together at the yellow table.

'Nothing like a juicy T-bone,' Frank told us – somewhat insensitively it occurred to me.

I mumbled something appropriate. Mollie accepted in silence what she must have considered a man's obvious privilege.

When Frank had lit his pipe and she and I were doing the dishes, she decided, 'Reckon you'd better stay the night. We can ring your folks in the mornin'.'

'Not too early. They don't like being disturbed early. Anyway, I think they've gone away. Yes, I remember some talk of their going on a journey.'

Mollie was burrowing into the dark looking for linen.

She took me into a little room, really the glassed-in end of a veranda, no space for more than a bed and a commode. It was lit by a brass lamp, something from off a ship. She made the bed. There was a smell of slightly damp sheets.

'You must be tired,' she told me.

I couldn't deny it. A big black green-eyed cat which had been observing me all the evening continued doing so. I could see that she, of all the household, was the only one who understood me.

'I love cats,' I told my hostess, then realised how sooky it must have sounded, so I added, 'I was probably a cat myself in a former existence.'

Mollie considered it beneath an answer. She showed me how to switch off the adapted ship's lamp.

'You promise you won't ring them too early. There's a lot I'd like to tell you.'

'No reason why we shouldn't have a yarn.'

'I'd like to dance for you, too.'

'Waddayerknow! You were a dancer, were yer?'

'Yes and no. I can do anything I put my mind to.'

The cat sat upright, positively Egyptian, watching my every thought.

'Any'ow, night night,' said Mollie.

'What's its name?'

'That's Mysie.'

'A good homely name.'

Mollie lumbered on her way leaving me destitute. The cat's tail brushed against me lightly, before, I imagined, going on the prowl. I could hear the Dobbins mumbling, yawning, doing things to their teeth, the springs of a bed answering their bodies.

I cry a little before realising I am not alone. You never are – are you really? Oh yes you are, desperately at times. But now the room is brilliantly lit. The ballroom of the Adolf Hitler Hotel, Washington DC. Hilary my husband and Henry his father have taken me with them on one of those mysterious business trips husbands and fathers-in-law indulge in. I send them down to the ballroom in advance because I have to prepare. They ask me what it is I have to do. 'Considering it's such an important occasion – this ball in aid of the needy – the unemployed – the persecuted – the whatever – I have to look my best, don't I? Do your position justice, don't I?' They agree, and go down without me.

I make myself look glorious in my Fortuny, its silken pleats so fine it will pass through the eye of a wedding ring. My hands tremble with excitement. Although the silk, of faintest, almost imperceptible silver clings to the breasts, the skirt can be made to swirl. I slip my feet into silver, winged sandals. I perfume the lobes of my ears. I paint my lips as delicately as a debutante's. Most important of all, I take up this basket, a common-or-garden affair used by peasant women in transporting their more precious wares, such as goat cheeses, or those big bruisable purple figs, to market. In my version of this crude basket I pile the deplorable mountain of my jewels. Their mineral splendours glower coldly back at me. Now I am ready.

I stand poised on the threshold of the ballroom. I can see Hilary and Henry seated on fragile gilt chairs beside a gilt table at the far end of the room. When I make my entrance the band leads the applause followed by all the diners who have bought tickets for this charity concern. I am superb.

Moulded to my breasts, the dress streams out behind me in the draught. I might have flown in from Samothrace the moment before. I kick off my no longer necessary winged sandals. I rise on my painted toes and float out across the glassy ballroom under my own impetus. I dance, and as I dance I sing (it could have been *I shook the flowering almond tree* ...) I can't resist reassuring myself how superb I am. In my miraculous swirling dress. Everyone is enraptured – excepting my two men, Hilary as livid as the morgue, a congested Henry suggesting a misshapen hamburger, as I whirl past them, scattering handfuls of jewels in the name of charity.

As the frozen American women seated on the sidelines with their business and politician husbands get the idea and begin to thaw, they drag off their jewels and fling them into the arena before husbandly hands start restraining them. Rid of my basketful, I tear a couple of star sapphires from my ears. I am panting somewhat unaesthetically by now, and Hilary and Henry have started crawling on all fours, trying to retrieve a personal fortune from the Adolf Hitler boards. Stuffing their pockets. While from either side advances the American herd of businessmen and politicians, snouts to the ground as though rootling after a rare crop of truffles.

I tread on what I see to be a diamond and sapphire spray (a birthday present from my father-in-law) and wound one of my heels quite severely. I am limping, blood trickling down the Fortuny corsage from my torn earlobes. I am led, always limping, away, to laughter and applause, the skitter of kettledrums diminishing, saxophones huffing, gulping, sighing for someone who can only be classed as a failure in the land of success.

Hanging back, I am dragged by Hilary and Henry, one each side of me.

I cry out, 'Leave me! Leave me!' But they won't.

God-knows-who locks me up in our Adolf Hitler suite.

'This is only a pill', they tell me, 'to sedate you.'

'In the morning', my men say, 'we shall see.'

When I awoke I was crying for the misunderstandings, the injustice in life. I was drenched with furry tears.

Suddenly I realised a cat, it could only have been Egyptian Mysie, was pissing spreadeagle on my face. In the Dobbins' glassed-in veranda room.

I flung her off. It was time to escape again.

I could tell where the worthy Dobbins might be found. In the distance there were snores, groans, the creaking of a bed.

I made my way, amongst furniture, finally arriving by touch at a great brass bedstead. I got down beside it, I lay there thankfully, for company, beside my dearest Dobbin parents. I subsided by degrees.

A noise of trees, sea, night and furniture, on the shores of almost sleep . . .

Till a horny foot trod down on ME. A *man* let out a snort, followed by a terrible fart.

Sheets were hissing off.

'Hey Frank wotissittwot . . .?'

'Arr, Moll – it's – I bet it's the one oo moved in – Mrs Nelly Wotnot!'

He trod forth farting worse then ever.

Lights.

Moll's hair was frizzed around her face.

Frank in a nightshirt. 'Gotter getter out of 'ere ter morrer. She's unreal.'

Mollie shushed her Frank and said, 'We both understand

46

yer, Nell, *but ...*'

The Egyptian cat sat looking at me. She might have been the guardian of Abu Simbel, not Dobbins' Mysie of Watson's Bay.

Mollie led me back to my room. 'You could have given Frank a turn, Nell. I don't know what got into you.'

'I was lonely. I wanted to be with my parents.'

'I don't know how as you can't spend a few hours on yer own, and seeing as I made you so comfortable – mi feather-stitched weddin sheets ...'

She began fussing with the bed.

'Blow me – you wet it too!'

As it was only the pillow, I wondered what athletics Mollie Dobbin visualised me getting up to in bed. She didn't give me time to explain that her wretched cat ... People don't believe, anyway.

'It's almost morning,' she said. 'I can't change you. You'll have to make do. Settle down as best yer can.' She switched the light off and went. Morning was certainly on its way. Grey was seeping. I did not know whether to feel glad or sad. I leaned my face against the cold pane. I had been returned to that limbo where I spend so much of my time. Nobody ever believes that inside an old woman there's a young girl waiting. I pressed my rounded mouth against the grey-washed window. Fresh from their roost in Neptune's Cave, gulls were starting to limber up with long slow sweeps of their aluminium wings. The grey distance was infused with red, the scarlet threads bringing to my mind the unhatched, shell-less eggs dragged from the innards of a slaughtered hen. My head bumped against the glass in time with all these revelations.

*   *   *

Later when Mollie and I had finished our cups of milky tea in the kitchen, I asked what had become of Frank.

'Frank's down the garden with 'is termarters. Pinchin' out the shoots.'

'Can't I help him? Can't I do something for somebody?'

'You must never ever intrude on Frank when 'e's with 'is termarters. He'd never forgive me. Termarters are holy in Frank's book.'

At that moment we heard him call out, 'Can't you winkle 'er number out of 'er?'

Mollie grunted. She didn't answer because she knew I must have heard.

'Frank's a very reasonable man,' she told me. 'He knows the only reasonable thing is for us to contact your family. You must know that,' she hesitated, 'because you're reasonable too.'

She had been assembling the wherewithal for baking bread. 'Eh, Nell? What about giving us yer telephone number? Yew must 'uv got it written down somewhere.'

'I haven't, I tell you. I lost my bag. Before I visit you next time, I'll have the number tattooed on my wrist.'

'Arr, Nell, you're a fair trimmer!'

She was breathing hard as she kneaded the dough. Her long white floury laundered apron nearly killed me with its cleanliness, its sweetness. She divided the dough, formed it into loaves, and arranged them in tins, to 'prove', she said. They looked to me like babies awaiting birth or burial. I could hardly restrain my sobs.

The cat no doubt thought me a fool. She had stretched herself full length at the back of the stove. She would never stop her green-eyed observation of me. She was the only cat – I think – who hadn't liked me. She had crooked one of her paws as though preparing to scoop a goldfish from under the water-lily pads.

I had to tell Mollie, 'Somewhere I think I heard about furry water-lilies.'

Mollie rubbed a cheek with a floury hand. 'There's a lot of funny things,' she admitted.

'What can I do?'

'Stay quiet,' she advised.

Had I been a nun I could have told my beads. I could have meditated if I had been a Buddhist. I could have done almost anything if I had an identity, like the furniture inside this house or dahlias the other side of the window. But I hadn't found the frame which fitted me.

That's rot of course. I've always become anything I intended to. Mollie Dobbin would have grasped that from all I had told her, so I stayed quiet as she advised for fear of making a fool of myself.

It must have been well into the morning, the loaves had proved themselves and gone inside the oven, and Mollie was sweeping the floor of her hygienic kitchen, when we heard the sound of a vehicle crunching over stones down the road which led from the upper reaches. The sound must have encouraged Frank to leave the company of his tomatoes. First his head, then his shoulders, appeared from the garden below.

Mollie flung aside her broom. I was struck cold by what might be preparing for me.

'It must be ... Yes, it is!' Mollie jerked at me over her shoulder as she hurried outside.

Very cautiously I followed. There was nothing else I could do. If I hid they would only drag me out, from under bed, or out of cupboard. If I ran up the hill in the direction of the Gap, they would catch me before I jumped.

It was the Great Booby of a cop who had charged me – yesterday, was it? or several days ago, now squeezing his swollen body out of a shiny paddy-wagon.

'They tell me you've got a visitor.'

Who told him, I wondered.

'That's right.' Grinning wider, Frank eased himself higher, out of his asylum, into the real world.

Mollie would have joined him in his affirmation (such people are the greatest joiners) if a second person had not been ejected from the paddy-wagon. She came round from the offside – my daughter Hilda in grey cotton gloves. The state of her emotions could be measured by her hatlessness. Otherwise, there was no sign of emotion on her little face: she was a Gray. I turned my own identifiable face away from the chorus waiting to accuse.

'Mrs Eleanor Shadbolt,' Mollie led the prosecution.

Hilda and the Booby exchanged glances, not to say smiles. Had something come into my Hilda's life in the shape of a Booby? Surely not; she was too great a snob.

'Never 'eard of a Shadbolt.' The policeman crunched any possibility of that into the drive.

Frank: 'That's what the lady told us.'

Hilda: 'She's my mother – Alexandra,' after embarrassed hesitations, she came up with a cough, a sigh, and a compromise, 'Gray is the family name.'

She sounded so cute and believable, my little daughter.

The Dobbins (in unison): 'Waddayerknow!'

I was exposed on all sides. I could only hold up my head for my throat to be slit or garrotted. At least there was a sky above with clouds and gulls sailing in it.

The cop thanked the Dobbins, so did my Hilda to a lesser degree; she is one of those who expect to receive rather than give thanks.

They climbed back inside the wagon, dragging and pushing their prey.

As they started up, the victim leaned out calling to her surrogate mother and reluctant dad, 'Thank you, thank you! I love you! You are my – more than friends – my family. Don't worry, I shall be back.'

The Dobbins waved. They wanted to do their best by one, but didn't believe anything of what I had said.

'Yes, yes,' they called, they waved. 'No doubt about it!' Frank's teeth were lying together, Mollie's giggles were knotted in her throat.

We waved, and might never have stopped, till Mollie let out a shriek.

'The bread! The bread!'

She tore inside, dragging her husband by a scabby wrist.

Hilda and the Booby were chuckling together, looking at each other. How much they understood about the burnt loaves, I wouldn't have known. Even less, probably, about the babies my surrogate mother and I had prepared for their holocaust.

Soon I was back home on the edge of the Park writing and writing as though nothing had happened (everything always has, of course, and a bit more). I have to catch up. At the same time I am protecting myself by cultivating this jungle of words. None of the Boobies will investigate me if I plait the branches densely enough. Does Hilda have continued contact with the prosecuting Booby of those days? I wonder. I listen for the telephone, but cannot arrive

at a firm conclusion. She comes in, on the pretext of bringing me marrrow-on-toast or a cup of bouillon. I curve an
arm around my work to protect it from the cheat who
needs my answers to pass her exam.

She goes. To report back to the Grand Seigneur of the
Sublime Porte. Little knowing what I know or what I
am.

She doesn't know I could have snitched her Booby from
under her nose, twitching off his jewelled turban with a
flick of the fingers. I could have dragged my surrogate
father Frank Dobbin by a horny hand into a bed of incest
if I had 'so desired', having learnt a trick or two from my
mother-in-law Magda Demirjian down the wrong end of
Smyrna. None of the Xenophon-Papapandelides would
have been seen dead talking to her on the Prokymaia had
she dared show herself in those parts – as the Smyrna
Breetish, the great Joneses and Llewellyns, the Burstalls and
the Brummages would not have recognised the Xenophons
and Pa-pa-pans within sight of St James's.

I know them all. I am them all. Most of all that snotty
little Jewess with the fly-encrusted eyelashes and nit-in-
fested hair, who saved her Jewish bacon by charming a
Gauleiter with her voice when she learned how to use it.

'She was the daughter of a carpenter, an honest Jew who
smelled of shavings and beeswax.'

Hilda always comes in if I happen to express my
thoughts aloud. 'I thought Magda was really the daughter
of Diacono, the Syro-Maltese station master at Benha.'

'Oh yes, she was that too.' Hilda ties knots in my gut
by knowing too much and not enough. 'I would love to
give a dinner party for all the people I have ever known.'

'Would they forgive you?'

'Probably not. But I would love to give it. I'd wear all my jewels. I'd wear ...'

'It's late, Mother. Shall I bring you a boiled egg?'

'Oh, yes, And hard. All your culinary science goes into the boiling of a hard egg – but *hard*.'

I know I am hateful, I cried awhile after she had gone to do the deed. Poor Hilda! She is one of my burnt offerings to the jealous god.

And Hal. It is time my son appeared. It is difficult to introduce Hal. He is so subtly camouflaged nobody but himself or his mother could have invented him. Deliberately I say 'invented' because I didn't just give birth to Hal. No ordinary mother could have had him. Mollie Dobbin, for instance, though she too had her troubles with Charlie from what she told me about the false amber necklace he sent her before he was torpedoed.

But Hal ...

All mothers think their sons have issued from their wombs. A son like Hal would never admit this, and I am ready to agree. We have never had this conversation and I expect we never shall. I might have it with old Patrick, who was, I suppose, my collaborator in, not so much inventing Hal, for I cannot deny he originated as Hilary's sperm, but as creators of the finished wretch. He was what Patrick and I both looked for as part of our complicated, many-faceted lives.

Hilda might announce, 'Patrick rang.'

'What about?' Too sharply by half.

'Hal. He thought you might like to see him.'

'If Hal wants to see me, surely he can come?'

'It isn't always as easy as that.'

'I know.'

She is looking at me in her little screwed-up way.

'When I was pregnant Patrick and I were listening on one occasion to *The Trojans*. We were holding hands. Hilary can't bear Berlioz. What he really goes for is Mahler – because Mahler is so full of self-pity.'

Hilda looks at me more closely than ever.

'Yes. I know what you're going to say – that your mother ... that Alma ... and the rest of it ... that when I was pregnant with Hal, it was Alexandria and no one would have heard of Berlioz, let alone played him, they were too busy getting on with adultery and bridge.'

When I begin to laugh, to retch, she goes away, leaving me to deal with my thoughts.

One day after I returned from my stay with the Dobbins, Hal appeared. I could sense he was materialising. There is that about a son like Hal and his relationship with a mother like me. There is no ringing of bells, it is like a change in the weather, winds veering, a fall in temperature, veils of cloud. So on this occasion I knew Hal was mounting the rise towards the veranda. I could feel a cool draught between my calves and the backs of my knees.

I was sitting writing in what I am vain enough to call my study, though I have studied practically nothing beyond my own intuition – oh, and by fits and starts, the Bible, the Talmud, the Jewish mystics, the Bhagavad Gita, various Zen masters, and dear old Father Jung who, I am told, I misinterpret. When I felt the draught that Hal's arrival creates, I put aside my pen. I knew I was relatively free, Hilda having gone off on some mysterious mission of her own. I opened the glass doors to the veranda. I had very little time in which to rehearse the approaching scene with my son. I could have turned on the mumsie act, he would have hated that, but so would I. Instead, knowing he would hate it equally, I played it cool.

'How's business?' I asked.

An aesthete, coming of a business line of Gray antique dealers, each performing the role more amateurishly than the last, he could only resent the remark. Certainly Hal carried on the business with enough flair to live tastefully. There was no more to it than that.

'Business!' His nostrils contracted at mention of the dirty word.

He had such a delicate nose there were occasions when I could have bitten it off and returned it to the womb of my imagination.

'Actually,' he said, coming inside, 'I've just picked up a very charming piece – an agate and silver-gilt snuff-box set with brilliants, said to have belonged to Lieselotte von der Pfaltz.'

'How very charming!'

'Actually, that isn't the whole provenance, it plays a little tune when opened – well, some German jingle, still to be identified.'

'Ending in a fart, surely.'

'Mother, you're everything the dreary Hilda says you are!'

'But Lieselotte was the Queen of Farts. She challenged her ladies and nobody dared outfart her.'

Hal subsided in what is almost the only comfortable chair. 'Pouf! What a ghastly fug in this den of yours.'

'Memory germinates in fug, I find.'

I was already weary of my son and could have returned to my writing, not without first brushing my lips, I have to admit, against his deliciously tended little moustache.

'May I kiss you – darling?' I ventured from behind my teeth (I could have bitten off nose, moustache, the lot).

'Kissing is out, Mum. So unhygienic.'

He dissolved into a laughter I recognised as mine and in which I joined him.

In spite of the Gray trademark, Hal was almost entirely me, descended from the Xenophons, the Papapandelides, and regrettably, from the other end of the scale, the Demirjian-Diacono-Bogdarlys, and many other crypto-relatives.

'What have you done with your friend?' I asked.

'My friend?' He parried the blow with a skilful twitch to the right.

'Father Whatever – Joel, isn't it? The Jewish priest.'

Hal sat with his legs thrust out straight in front of him, his chin sunk in an exquisite Roman cravat held in place by a turquoise ring.

'Father Joel', his mouth formed the word 'Father' with the greatest reverence, 'is a very spiritual man. His regret is that I am not a Christian, his hope that I may turn.'

Did I see the Jewish priest's blue-shaven jaws glitter in the dusk beyond the hibiscus, as he waited patiently to continue proselytising his lover?

Hal jumped up from his no longer easy chair. 'But I am not his lover!'

'Who accused you? Or did you plug into my thoughts, my poor darling boy? Everybody needs a lover, a father, a God. I'm only in doubt about a mother.'

The scene might have ended in worse knots if Hilda hadn't come in. 'You must have wondered where I was,' she began like most unwanted people. 'I found it was late-night shopping. Quaker Oats was on the special.' She shook her plastic bag in a gesture of triumph.

Hal let out a moan, and stamped off, slamming the glass doors behind him. As Hilda remarked, he could have smashed them.

'He's gone to join the priest.'

'The who?'

'I believe his name is Morgenstern – "Morning Star" if you must know.'

'Never heard of him. But what a lovely name.'

'That's what Herman Wouk thought.'

It was wasted on her. She had gone to deposit the rolled oats in one of those corners of the pantry only she has ever explored. Hilda has her pantry. I am stranded again on the shores of memory and the detritus of what I imagine as future.

I must never let Hilda see I envy her, but I do. She is *self-satisfied*. She has achieved all she ever aspired to. I don't think she aspired to a man. I believe she is a virgin in spite of that conspiracy with the Great Booby of the Police Force. She may have aspired to Patrick, but he let her down lightly. Whereas I who have had men, women too, have never been consummated in a true sense. During the sleepless hours I am a failure. I hate myself because I know the inner me. My beauty is a mask, my writing a subterfuge.

Once in the night I jumped up and looked at myself. I encountered a ravaged ghoul, member of an order to which I had never belonged in memory, Sisters of the Sacred Blood. It was dripping from my mouth. At every level above this limbo of vampires, I had failed. In the order to which I had been admitted, I like to think, at one stage of memory, my vocation was a farce, on looking back. Finbarr of the farmyard, who tended the chooks and piglets, who renewed the water for the stinking ducks, was more acceptable in the eyes of Reverend Mother and God. She had freckled hands caked with pollard and bonemeal. She had a squint. I believe the others all saw through me, but accepted Benedict as a joke. My dignity never atoned for my duplicity – I believe only Bernadette ever saw the worth I hoped might be found in me and this through the age and sanctity Bernadette herself had achieved. Possibly the sanctity of innocence. I loved her, as I loved our old Smaragda, the nurse from Smyrna.

After I got back into my bed the whole potful of dreams was boiled up together. Smaragda's kerchief, pollarded hands, the green, slimy duck water steaming with the laughter of vampire nuns.

I was released exhausted at first light yet refreshed in a sense. I was sitting at my dressing-table combing out my hair when Hilda brought me a bowl of coffee and some rusks.

'You know coffee is poison,' she said. 'You really ought to give it up.'

'I've been poisoned often and never died.'

She dragged at the curtains to let in more light and expose her mother.

She said, 'Your hair is falling out. We must do something about it. At this rate you'll be bald as a nun in another six months.'

'Is that a rational remark, Hilda, from one who likes to think herself a rationalist. And what do you know about nuns.'

'Well, I've read and heard about them. And what do you know, anyway?'

'I was with them all night. Much of my life, for that matter. You, my rationalist daughter can't understand I have a vocation – of sorts. As an average Australian you find that faith, let alone a vocation, would be too demanding.'

She subsided into thoughtfulness.

I went into the bathroom to brush my teeth. My gums bared at the glass were bleeding. I threw down the toothbrush.

I must accept that my daughter thinks I am mad.

I have my writing. But once again I realise I must escape from custody – prove my innocence.

Notes

p. 17   Panayia: the Greek Virgin Mary

p. 21   the Catastrophe: sack of Smyrna by the Turks in 1922

p. 24   Arachova: village near Delphi

p. 33   ... the Union and the Cecil: leading Alexandrian restaurant and hotel, no more than 500 yards apart

p. 34   Mazarita: suburb of Alexandria
      Bolonaki whisky: a local brew
      Prokymaia: quay at Smyrna

p. 44   Fortuny: Spanish-born Italian designer (1871–1949) Madrazo became Mariano. Fortuny is associated with Venice, where there is a museum honouring his work

p. 52   Grand Seigneur: the Sultan
      Sublime Porte: Constantinople
      St James's: Court of St James's, London
      saved her Jewish bacon by charming a *Gauleiter*: alludes to a certain Smyrna Jewess said to have associated with Goering

Editor's Intrusion

As editor of Alex Gray's memoirs it embarrasses me to interrupt them. But there are points at which it becomes unavoidable, and this is one.

Hilda had phoned me and asked more desperately than ever for help in dealing with her mother. Though I had known Hilda from babyhood we had never really seen inside each other. I had felt the baby fingers possessing one of mine like little pink caterpillars, the sea anemone mouth moistly pressed against my own. I had experienced the recoil of the adolescent girl, then recognised the ploys of womanhood: the coils or curtain of freshly washed hair offered to one she saw as more than a long-lasting friend – a man. I even considered from time to time what might have turned out another disastrous relationship. It could have been what she wanted. To replace the prime disaster of her life – her relationship with her mother.

Anyway, on this occasion she rang me and said, 'I've got to see you. She's gone again. I can't stand any more of it. Wait ...' (I could hear her closing a door.) 'This time she's taken a suitcase. God knows where she'll end up. She intends more than a walk to Watson's Bay.'

'I'll come at once,' I promised.

'No. Not here.' Her breathing grew more intense. 'I've got to get out of this house for a little.'

I wasn't all that pleased to have to put aside my work,

but arranged to meet her near the flower stall opposite the bank at the lower end of Martin Place. My work! Shoving it into a drawer of my desk, I wondered whether it could be of any account. Insistent characters like Hilda, Alex, Hilary, Magda make you suspect their lives count for more than the flesh and blood of your own creating.

Hilda was standing hatless, coatless, gloveless, against a background of ranunculus, cornflowers, gypsophila, and the tight rosebuds of any season. From a distance she looked frail, young, appealing. As one approached she began to wither slightly, till in close-up she became a solitary spinster, who still might have had appeal for those who cherish the nostalgic image of crushed muslin and Lillian Gish. She smiled. She took my arm and squeezed it to reassure me of her support. (By now I had taken to walking with a stick as arthritis was invading my feet.) We must have suggested to anyone who bothered to notice an uncle with a niece or an elderly guy with a sympathetic woman friend. They would not have looked long enough to work out who was guiding who – in the idiom of our day. Anyhow, Hilda and I might not have agreed on the tactics of our relationship this bright morning in Martin Place.

We sat down in a café-snackery of the type which has proliferated over the years along mid-George Street without improving in quality or altering the general style. We both ordered straight black. But Hilda called after the waitress and changed to *cappuccino*.

She told me, 'I feel I need a touch of froth,' tracing with a fingernail a vague path through sugar spilt by a previous customer.

'When you rang me you told me she had gone.'

Breathlessly, 'Yes.'

'Then why did you close the door before we continued our conversation?'

'Habit, I suppose. Alex plugs into your thoughts.'

'And you into hers? It's not uncommon – two people at close quarters.'

She gave a grudging little laugh. 'Yes.'

'But had she left already? with this suitcase you mentioned.'

The waitress, a gaunt creature in straight hair and a wedding ring, had brought our coffees, slopping the frothy *cappuccino*. As the woman was leaving, Hilda seemed to be pleading with her to stay.

'What an inquisition, Patrick.'

'I'm only trying to get to the bottom of what you're telling me – work out a plan of action for the future.'

Hilda, for her part, was harder at work tracing a path through the spilt sugar, till halted by the *cappuccino* lake.

'You say she was packing a suitcase. Is Alex strong enough to go down and open the garage door and fetch a suitcase? I know you have a whole garageful of luggage left over from the various Gray travels.'

'Not those. They're full of cockroaches and mould. There's one I keep in a cupboard in my room – in case one of us has to go to hospital ...'

'That's practical – that's like you, Hilda.'

'... or go away ... *leave* ...'

'It was yours – the emergency suitcase Alex took with her?'

Hilda did not answer at once.

'I've reached the point where I can't stand any more, Patrick. Mother must be committed.'

'We've been through all this before. I've tried to persuade you. We must get in touch with Falkenberg.'

She hung her head. 'No! No!' Some undignified bubbles appeared on her lips. 'You don't understand. She's my mother.'

'Better one of you in a straitjacket than two. Let's be reasonable at least. You, Hilda, I thought were the most reasonable person on earth.'

'I love her. That's what you can't understand.'

'But darling . . .'

'Don't use that word! She's made it dirty.'

Describing one great arc, she swept the sugar, the slops, off the table. 'Let's get out of here,' she said.

I paid the straight-haired waitress, who had been observing us more disapprovingly every minute.

Across the street, Hilda bought a bunch of ranunculus, then a second. 'She loves them,' she said, looking radiant in every premature crease of her Lillian Gish face.

We walked away. I hailed a taxi.

'No,' she said, 'I'll take a bus, to return to normal. I mustn't let her know Falkenberg was anywhere near the surface of my mind.'

I wish I could serve Hilda better. I am not even a mentor.

I spent a delicious morning with myself, my writing. I heard Hilda go out to some dreary rendezvous with some-one – Patrick? Hal? the Jewish priest? When she returned, I heard the key, sleeker than usual, in the lock. She closed the door very carefully. She may have oiled the lock before going out.

Does Hilda know that the key to anybody is in one's self?

I waited for her. I had come down to Hilary's study. She stood inside the door, holding a bunch of ranunculus. They lit her little wrinkled face.

'I brought you these, Mummy. I know you adore them.'

I got up and took them from her.

'Is "adore" *your* word, Hilda? I love them – yes.' It was devious of me to reject the word 'adore', so often my own.

As I crushed the flowers against my breasts I turned to face the audience, and the spot hit me as squarely as the waves of applause.

I bowed my head with the humility, the warmth, ex-pected of a great actress.

I laid the ranunculus on a console. Hadn't they served their purpose?

'How did you get on, darling, with whichever of them it was?'

'I had a coffee in town with Patrick.'

'And find me still here.'

'I can't deny I thought you were preparing something.'

'Something in a suitcase.' I know about the one she keeps in her wardrobe.

Hilda didn't answer.

'I haven't any need for suitcases. I've been there and back while you and Patrick were plotting the future over mediocre coffee in George Street.'

This time I wouldn't be able to show her blisters on my feet. My walk to Watson's Bay was something Hilda the archivist could envisage. Besides, she had found me at the Dobbins' cottage and no doubt recorded all. But the great flights my temperament requires and my state of mind allows are something she will never imagine.

However, there is a clue she pounces on immediately; my chinchilla coat lying in a heap on the carpet.

'What on earth ...?' She picks it up and dusts it down. 'You haven't worn it for years.'

'That doesn't mean I shouldn't wear it if I feel like it. I did, so I got it out of the mothbag.'

'Chinchilla by daylight! I'd have thought you'd be the first to consider that vulgar.'

'Not if it's for a vulgar occasion.'

She hurried to return the coat to its mothballs. Poor old practical Hilda! She had never been able to appreciate the sensuousnesss of that chinchilla coat. To understand my need to take off my clothes and feel it against my nakedness, snuff up its luxury, mothballs and all, through dilated nostrils.

I had worn it on many occasions, some of which I would call vulgar – Cairo, Washington, London, Paris. Once, in Stockholm – I think it was – I slit it with the mother-of-pearl pocket fruit-knife I had given Hilary for one of our anniversaries (I loved to watch him after peeling a ripe peach, the juice running from his full lips) and here I was slashing with my mother-of-pearl token of love the chinchilla coat to show my contempt for, my hatred of all superfluous possessions. My chinchilla – I wept for it afterwards – had to be rushed to a furrier. Yes, it was Stockholm. I stood naked at the open window, above the lights and water, the ferries and the islands, hoping I might catch pneumonia. Hilary slammed the window shut. I was surprised by his suddenly vicious authority. We made love on a cold sheet. The buttons of his suit gouged me. The incident real enough for Hilda to record. She would have had a high old time.

What she would not have understood was my flight this morning as she sat trafficking with her accomplice in a George Street coffee shop.

When she had left for her assignation I rummaged for the funds Hilda my banker did not know about, and stuffed a wad of notes down the top of my stocking. My thigh acquired a sense of independence my body and mind enjoyed only in writing and dreams. I didn't bother much about dress, only threw the chinchilla over a little, crumpled, grey frock.

I called a taxi and gave the address at which I calculated the party would soon be in full swing. The driver was a nondescript but not unacceptable man. I might have met him earlier in life somewhere in the Middle East. But I refused myself the luxury of fossicking through the past, perhaps ending on some Aegean rock, my liver pecked at by a great predatory bird, its beak shaped like a scimitar.

We reached the gate. I delved into my stocking and

brought out a handful of notes. The taxi-driver could hardly believe something wasn't expected of him. Or else I was mad. So many people think I am mad.

As he hesitated over the money I said, 'Well, why not? Isn't money for providing joy? Otherwise what's the point of it?'

It had never brought me joy, but I stick to the theory.

I got out, leaving the driver looking dazed, and addressed the security intercom.

The voice asked, 'Yes – who shall I announce?'

I replied, 'The Avenging Angel,' thus minimising my chances of admission.

I did not care, but after a chorus of titters the door opened, and I was let in. I mounted the marble steps to the tessellated porch, its pillars hung about with baskets of orchids.

I was received by a manservant in the English style. 'Is milady expecting you?'

I adopted my best swagger inside my expensive chinchilla coat. 'I'm always expected when I arrive.'

The butler was a bit astounded. 'What name shall I announce, madam?'

'The Empress Alexandra of Byzantium and Nicaea.'

The man was perturbed.

'Don't worry,' I assured him, 'I'm used to the company of property developers, newspaper proprietors, drug pushers, and political leaders – all the plastic riffraff of life. Otherwise how could I have survived?'

I had confused the butler so thoroughly he began leading me through the house, not without backward glances to see what I might be getting up to. I was simply assessing its contents: the chandeliers, the Aubusson carpet, the recently painted portraits of its owners (so recent the paint looked tacky on the canvas) along with a few ancestral portraits so unrelated they must have been picked up at auction. I could not have done anything about these works of art, but the unhappy butler would not have put it past me to hide a few jewelled snuff-boxes and Venetian ashtrays inside my coat. My last attempts at shoplifting had led to such embarrassment, I had given the profession away, but I couldn't very well tell the man that.

As we penetrated deeper into all this sumptuousness, a lady began advancing towards me from the opposite end. Without her coronet of hair and her self-assurance she would have appeared dumpy. As it was, her aura of wealth and a shift embroidered with seed-pearls helped her float. Behind her there trailed across tiles and rugs a seemingly endless pigtail with strings of the ubiquitous pearls plaited into it.

The butler rose to the occasion more or less, in a tormented stutter. 'The Empress Alexandra of Byzantium and Nicaea, milady.'

Milady took my hand in her pudgy ones. She dimpled in one of her olive cheeks.

'So charming of you to honour us, darling heart. Rather early, but we can enjoy a chat, can't we?'

I had read so often about Lady Miriam Surplus of Comebychance Hall I knew her as intimately as I would have known a sister.

Continuing to play her game, she said, 'Alexandra ...? From my reading – I adore history – I thought you would be Theodora.'

'That old fake! Circus rider, and prostitute into the bargain.'

We understood each other perfectly: our laughter sealed a bond.

She began stroking my coat. 'Such fine pelts. To tell the truth my late father was a furrier. Well, why not? Aren't we a democratic country? Up to a point, of course. Royalty is so decorative.'

Together we did an about turn, during which Milady frowned the butler out of existence, and I narrowly missed stepping on the trailing pigtail as we moved towards the garden.

In the last of the reception rooms there loomed a grey figure in black leotards who avoided me more dexterously than I Lady Miriam's trailing pigtail.

'This is my darling Wilton,' she explained. 'He's more a philosopher and poet than one for silly luncheon parties, unless for the leftovers when we settle down to them *en famille*. Just now he's trying to reconcile classical ballet with gravity.'

To demonstrate, Sir Wilton focused the intruder with a grey stare, and on executing a mad *fouetté*, disappeared into the wings.

Slaves had been laying tables in the garden beside the water: the little gold tables and spindly chairs which furnish the social lives of such as Lady Miriam. There was also a long, laden buffet on which those unwanted guests the blowies were settling here and there.

We went out. The invited, and perhaps a few crashers, were arriving. I should have felt more at home from reading about them almost as frequently as I had read about their hostess. But the familiarity of each guest with Miriam of Comebychance dared any other familiar, let alone an outsider like myself, to usurp the favoured position they enjoyed. As for Miriam, she held the balance by rubbing up against their pride, by darl-ing them along without distinguishing one darl from another.

Benny Glick had only recently bought his way out of gaol. Sir Yuri Kiss had not yet gone in. His wife Pearlie could not have been well, she was so irritable, still flicking, as it were, the little whip, stamping a tattoo in the red boots she had once worn in cabaret. 'If I leave you, Yuriko,' she warned between pouts, 'you must not be surprised.' 'But what more can you expect, Piri? You have your own white Rolls, your speedboat, trips to New York, Paris, Switzerland – and Surfers. Your life as you like to live it.' 'What else do I expect Yuriko? A kiss!'

Benny Glick at least had not brought any wives or strumpets, his life was renewable at any moment, at any party.

'Who's the old girl in the chinchilla?' he asked his hostess.

'If you only knew!'

'Old arms, old breasts. Nothing wrong with the chinchilla.'

Lady Miriam's experience and constitution would help her survive such an indigestible brew of guests. More trying than anything perhaps was the expression on the face of Elwyn Nosh. She could tell from a distance he was preparing to write off her lobster mousse with its sieved sauce of sour cream and mango and garnish of truffles and oysters. Elwyn more than anyone might poison her reputation.

Early, hungrier, thirstier guests were clotting in groups between potted-out flowerbeds, downing Scotch or champers, stuffing in the caviar and chicken livers, trying out an uneasy stance on the trampoline lawns. The lady in Thai silk fell backwards into the cinerarias (' ... poor thing, she's diabetic ...')

A large young woman from the Opera was having a go at the 'Liebestod' as a form of entertainment. The chorus on the lawns was forced to amplify its voice and increase its already enthusiastic intake of savouries till the litter of toothpicks might have provided material enough for a communal game of spillikins.

The guests continued pouring in: artists hopeful of patronage, dressmakers, milliners, actors and singers with futures ahead of them, telly crews, and gossip writers.

The Boy Scout was there in his Baden-Powell pyramid, his tea-rose wife deliciously smelling of Elizabeth Arden. Desperate young girls prepared to accept marriage with whichever atrophied barrister proposed.

To a clatter of hooves on marble steps, Sir Wilton's niece the Hon. Joan Scott Tupper (' ... ex-wife of Tony, y'know, Lord Pinchbeck's heir who crossed the floor ...') rode her dappled mare, Sieglinde, into the Comebychance garden. 'Scottie' looked sonsy in the extreme, in her black velvet hunting cap, lace jabot, and ruffles. Dismounting, she handed the reins to a Filipino houseboy, ill at ease with such a handful as the farting, over-stuffed mare. 'Scottie' too, looked over-stuffed, but managed to stuff in a handful of cheese crescents while her mare chewed on a broccoli salad.

'Popped in for a bit to sustain me on the ride,' 'Scottie' spluttered at her aunt, while automatically forcing her swag of blonde curls into the aunt's riper than usual olive cheek.

Miriam accepted these rites with well-rehearsed humility.

Benny Glick was eyeing 'Scottie', who obviously did not fancy offers from that direction. As the party progressed, body cannoned off body into fresh combinations of the same game. Shrubberies invited exploration. Assisted by a dwarf bass, the stout young woman from the Opera had thrown herself into 'Brunnhilde's Farewell'.

Finally I got the giggles which, I gathered from sideways glances, several discreetly corseted matrons diagnosed as hiccups.

'May I bring you something? A glass of water?' the Boy Scout's lady asked. 'Or perhaps a sliver of slippery elm?'

But I knew I was beyond cure, unless through the therapy of revolutionary violence.

I grabbed Sieglinde's bridle from the hands of the Filipino strapper. I leaped at the saddle, only briefly fumbling for the stirrups. I was again astride in all the glory of my rights as Empress and circus rider.

Sieglinde pigrooted once or twice before responding to the master touch. Back and forth I rode her, above trestles littered with the shambles of Miriam's luncheon, ploughing the Double Bay hair-dos, the bald pates, the hair-pieces and blow-waves, then down to the plastic scum where beach meets lantana, and up again, up. I might have been leading a cohort in which Valkyries galloped neck and neck with Sisters of the Sacred Blood. We skimmed the spires of cypresses, scattering nests and fledglings of spinebill and bulbul, till in the act of wheeling, Sieglinde stumbled on the transverse branch of a deodar. She dumped me just short of the buffet's ruined conceits. It was a soft landing. Could have been on a heap of horse-turd, I reasoned as I closed my ears to Miriam's screams of, 'Get her out of here, someone – whoever she is ...'

When I re-opened my eyes pandemonium must have been at its peak. I noticed I was tightly holding on to Lady Miriam's detached pigtail. There was nothing for it but to regain unconsciousness.

When Hilda came back into the room I felt I had to apologise for the state my chinchilla must be in.

She seemed mystified. 'Perfect condition. Though I wouldn't wear them – on principle – I've got to admit furs have a glamour of their own.'

'You didn't notice anything – not even a smell?'

'Only mothballs.'

'But there must have – from my landing in the horse-shit . . .'

She didn't even blink. She said she was going into the garden to turn the sprinklers on. I was glad to be left alone. I could get on with my writing without further argument.

I have done this little drawing of the island in the margin. The sea in which it lies suggests a sheet of glass, when in fact the seas which surround Nisos are almost always troubled. The island is elongated, damp and melancholy, smelling of pine trees, extinguished candles, stale incense and cooking oil stagnating round left-over food.

Often in the night I hear a gunshot, for there are suicides on Nisos. Murders too, by Turks, pirates, guerrillas, lovers. Or is the shot I hear from the murder I committed in killing Hilary's spaniel, Danny? Hilary's own death was silent. I suppose one would call it suicide, technically anyway, only a half-murder. Nor does it belong to Nisos, rather the island on which we lived, live still, beside the Park.

I call out through my sleep to this body gradually forming beside me in the bed. It is not Hilary but Onouphrios,
who answers, or more precisely grunts his way into my
dream like the gross human pig that he is. A heavy boar.
(I shan't be tempted by the obvious pun which offers itself.)
A man can be disarming. But a male, never, thrashing
around, bristles sprouting, prickling, cutting, as he thrusts
in the direction his desire is leading him.

Smooth and civilised, Hilary was misguided in another
way. In the early days of our marriage he liked to refer to
desire as love. I did too, for that matter. We did not believe
we were being deceitful. We weren't either. Were we? We
couldn't have been. The children were living proof of our
bona fides. We were sincere. We believed in our vocation
as parents.

Even though we are unconscious of it, we are all born
to search for a vocation. Hilda and Hal? Probably in their
own perverted way.

Like Onouphrios the monk. Otherwise would he rise
from the bed in the middle of the night, disentangle himself
from the sweaty sheet, which has practically strangled us,
and stagger into the chapel to uphold his Orthodox faith?
Even I, in my shabby habit, am moved to tears by the
sublime mumblings as Onouphrios performs the office
under the Pantocrator's eye. Myself always in the shadows.
I was nothing. I *am* nothing. Cassianí the nun, who sweeps
the mouse droppings, the fallen nests, the broken tiles, out
of the chapel of Ayia Ekaterini at Nisos, for the resump-
tion of its spiritual life, to the glory of the Pantocrator, the
Panayia, and their Saints.

It was some time before the Abbot dropped to what had
happened. Panaretos, I could see, was a cynic. That thin

smile. On coming down from the Monastery he held out a hand for me to kiss. It smelled of rose-water sprinkled over sweating lard. I kissed the hand, the ring. In contrast with the flabby flesh, the ring was brutally direct. It bruised my lip.

After the Abbot's inspection, and apparent approval, Onouphrios and I became the servants of Ayia Ekaterini, one of whose eyes had been gouged out by vandals. I did not see Panaretos again. But his smile lingered, enjoying the situation he had created by allowing this nun to set up house with his representative Onouphrios.

From time to time the monk went up to the Monastery. Whether he indulged in the Abbot's unnatural pleasures of which the more sophisticated townspeople spoke, I had no proof. I suspect Panaretos despised the rough, stinking peasant turned monk. For his part, the monk may have pandered to his superior by encouraging his vice and taking part in his sexual orgies. Onouphrios valued his independence, and the services Cassianí provided.

The church of Ayia Ekaterini became a favourite sight for foreign tourists on their way up to the Monastery, probably less for its inferior, damaged architecture than the mystery of its custodians. While Onouphrios was pointing out architrave and fresco, the visitors' eyes showed greater interest in the nun sweeping the tessellated floor, or bent above the vegetables she tended at a stone's throw from the church.

I was proud of my purple eggplant and emerald peppers, less of the worm-eaten cabbages. It did not bother me that my nails were black with honest dirt. When the visitors had satisfied their curiosity as far as possible they would cast a last long look at the nun weeding her plot. They could not undress me. My neglected face, made sallower by its frame of dark kerchief, gave them their only glimpse of flesh, possibly deepening the mystery of the monk and nun in charge of this dilapidated church. The tourists some-times left sums of money for its upkeep. Those who made substantial contributions Onouphrios entertained with little cups of coffee which he had me serve on an iron table covered with plastic in the space between the church and our quarters. Some of our guests, grimacing as they reached the bitter dregs at the bottom of the cup, would try to draw out the silent nun, with phrases in clumsy Greek. But Cassianí was either too discreet, or more prob-ably too stupid, to let them engage her in conversation. She might titter slightly to appease them, while veiling unexpectedly blue eyes behind dark lids.

Sometimes I used to escape, not along the path which linked our humble church with the Monastery, but by a less defined track which forked from the well-worn path-way just beyond our precinct, and wound around the shoulder of the mountain in a southerly direction. On most of these occasions Onouphrios would stand calling after me to return. If I looked back I could see the scowl that had formed on the yellow cheeks above the great black beard. He was afraid I might defect. Usually I ignored him, but sometimes I called back, knowing that the wind would convert my reply into nonsense.

I was what is known as 'free', stooped scuttling against the wind, over the stones, almost horizontal with the droughty earth and thistles. My feet in their peasant san-dals seemed scarcely to touch the ground. The south of Nisos, compared with other quarters of this moist and seductive island, was turned into a desert place by the hot

76

winds blowing out of Africa, out of Egypt directly to the south. I re-lived a former life on this barren hillside smelling of dust. I bit the tails of my hair escaped from under the kerchief. I stumbled readily and fell. I rolled over, grinding my back into the stones, face to face at last with the sky – dare I say Heaven, as opposed to the damp and mouldy simulacrum in our church, closer than I could hope to come to the saint's ecstasy on this hump-backed mountain, not always as barren as it seems, when in spring the earth breaks out in cyclamen and cistus, and the glowing spires of asphodel which draw one back to the world of reason with their stench of bed-bugs.

This evening I can feel the little bubbles of laughter coming in the gaps between my teeth. Laughter too can sanctify.

All kinds of herbs and bitter weeds grow on the mountain. I would dig up plantain and dandelions and stuff them into the prickly goat-hair *tagari* I always carry with me on these sorties. Goats often appear around me in a scampering of hard pellets. This evening a little doe in kid, scarcely more than a kid herself, butts my ribs before curvetting away into the wind.

I wander as far as the ruins of Hera's temple fenced with barbed wire against intruders. Only official guides have the key to the gate, which they unlock when they come with their mobs of tourists. I have no difficulty crawling through a goat-made hole in the wire – and come across the torso of the *kouros*. The portable archaeological finds have been moved to the museum in Athens. Why they overlooked the *kouros* torso is a mystery, unless he was left for my coming. Or is he in fact lying here, his ropes of hair and flattened nose, amongst the thistles? Has my psyche, perhaps, conjured him out of an existence we shared in Alexandria, Luxor, or Abu Simbel? Shivering with recognition, I run a finger over the square nipples.

On returning to the outside world, leaving on the barbed fence tufts of wind-blown hair, I find the little doe, my familiar, waiting for me on the slope. On all fours, I face her, eye to eye, forehead butting forehead, the tassels at her throat trembling, her belly stirring with the unborn kid. I caress the little teats, the udder already preparing milk. As I make for the church of Ayia Ekaterini, the goat trots beside me. I wonder how Onouphrios will receive her.

He is in the worst temper, expecting the meal I should have cooked him. My familiar has wisely removed herself. At times I heard pellets pattering on the tessellations in the nave of the church. On going to the kitchen door, I knew from the movement, the rustling in a clump of elders that she must be browsing there. Once I heard her tear a strip from the plastic cover on the iron table at which Onouphrios entertained his more generous guests. It made me happy to know she was occupied.

I go back to my own occupation, stewing a mess of eggplant and peppers for my master in some of the votive oil brought him by Kyria Vaso, widow of a tavernkeeper at the *skala*.

Vaso is devoted to Onouphrios, believing his hands responsible (with divine assistance of course) for the remission of arthritic pains in one of her legs. Ayia Ekaterini is famous for miraculous cures, witness the votive limbs, breasts, heads, in silver (or tin) suspended round the appropriate altar. In my half-sleep I often hear the whispered prayers of the sufferers reach out towards the bed in which I lie.

Tonight we are more down to earth. Onouphrios sits scoffing the mess of vegetables stewed in Vaso's rancid oil. Wasn't I eating? I tell him I will boil some of the *horta* I dug up on my walk, they would be more to my taste.

'Wind-makers!'

'They purify the blood.'

'If that's what you need.' His superiority over the weeds and herbs of the mountain did not prevent him letting out a belch.

I should add that another of his admirers, a peasant *ambelourgikós*, keeps him supplied with a rough red, the effects of which reverberate through the night.

On finishing his meal he went outside to make water. 'What's this?' I hear him shout.

I knew without prolonged investigation he had caught sight of the little parti-coloured doe slipping through the shadows cast by pine and elder.

'Could be a ghost. It's a night for ghosts.'

Suggestions of this kind, which he had not originated, tended to infuriate Onouphrios. 'What do you think you are?'

'I shan't say a nun – unless a failed one. A woman – as you ought to know.'

He was racked with laughter and Costa's rasping wine.

'I ought and do!' he coughed. Then quietened, 'You know what *they* say you are?'

'Who?'

'All the Christians from hereabouts.'

I knew what was coming. It would be just as they tell you in another world, 'You can only be mad. If you weren't, you couldn't say or do the things no normal woman says or does.'

I wait for Onouphrios to come out with his Greek version. 'You are a foreign devil. You have evil powers . No one in these parts has a *blue* eye.'

Having said his piece, he goes inside and falls on the bed.

I could not bring myself to follow. I walked round the solid, to some extent re-assuring mass of the church, and presently heard a crying from what I took to be the doe. She had lain down in the elder grove on a bed of pine-needles and had begun her labour. I soothed her straining sides. I helped deliver the kid, while the mother nibbled at my sleeve. I parted the bloodstained caul for the doe to infuse her offspring with life, which she did by licking, snuffling, bleating encouragement. The kid twitched and breathed. I bowed my head beneath the starry night for what I was vain enough to see as my own contribution to the continuity of being – though impostor-nun, sorceress, failed wife-mother, mere woman, in my various allotted lives.

Because I had nowhere else to go, I was drawn back to my mentor-lover. I lay down beside the monk and awaited what might be expected of me. I felt heavier than my actual body, my stone head and plaited locks weighing down the straw-filled pillow, my torso, and my rigid arms and thighs up to where they had been broken off, catching on the coarse sheet. Onouphrios rolled over against me and away, his breath hissing as his fingers touched square nipples carved out of stone.

'Lord in Heaven!' His high-pitched scream must have reached the ears of his superior at the Monastery.

Returned to my human form, I thought I heard the monk's scream echoed back as an inhuman wail.

The hour had come for us to present ourselves to the

Pantocrator, but this morning Onouphrios conducted a slobbered, indistinct version of the office.

With indifference I awaited daylight and the inevitable accusations. To pass the time I visited Meera, the secret name I had given my little doe. As I came near the place where she was hidden, the sounds I heard were calmly domestic in tone. The kid stood rocking on his pins, while the mother nuzzled and coaxed him to enjoy her teats. Our work was done.

Light as soft as feathers had begun drifting amongst the leaves. The age of peace could be dawning on earth. Then my pulses, my blood began to throb with the return of evil, nothing super-natural, but a viciousness projected by the human voice when accusing any individual suspected of possessing the evil eye, or some poor victim for whom it is decided the straitjacket is justified.

From the direction of the *skala* there were sounds of movement, a thrumming of voices broken by an occasional shout. I looked for Onouphrios, but could not find him, not that he was likely to defend a woman he despised. Had he left for the Monastery perhaps, hoping the Abbot might dismiss terrors the night had generated in him?

Seized with a rage against the hopelessness and the hypocrisies of humankind, I armed myself with my goat-hair *tagari* and started snatching the votive offerings from where they hung above the Saint's altar. I stuffed the metal tokens into the *tagari* and rushed from the church towards the mountain, now rapidly forming in the morning light. As I ran, one arm squeezing the *tagari* to my side, the votive plaques gave out a twittering, a sighing, like a bagpipe's dying breath.

Some way up the mountain, I must have fallen, either

from exhaustion or in a kind of fit. The light was fairly solid by the time I came to my senses and began to gather up my bruises, scratches and downright wounds from falling amongst the stones and thistles.

Steadying myself on all fours, I realised I was not alone. A goat army was rallying round me, horned and shaggy, their hard hooves drumming the harder earth. Their grave yellow eyes accepted those of a human being rejected by the 'Christians' of Nisos.

We formed up and marched down the mountain in the direction of Ayia Ekaterini.

The rival forces confronted one another in an atmosphere of confusion and the smell of burning flesh. I guessed what had happened from the desperate cries of Meera. On what had been my vegetable patch, Onouphrios stood tearing apart and devouring the kid's burnt flesh. Around him an array of townspeople and peasants pointing in my direction, at my back the goat army from the mountain.

The humans were shouting. 'The Eye! The Eye! She put the Eye on His Holiness Panaretos.'

Normally they would not have given a bugger (in blunt terms) for their pederast Abbot, only here was the foreigner, the blue-eyed witch, who could be held responsible. Panaretos, one gathered from the mob's hysterical exchanges, had been strangled during the night – probably murdered by some of the boys he had misused.

While Onouphrios stood, a Moloch tearing the kid's charred flesh with his ugly 'Christian' teeth, I closed my eyes. Through the confusion of curses and smoke, the votive plaques in the *tagari*, which I still held squeezed against my ribs, set up their wheezy, metallic twitter . . . If return-

ing the stolen tokens to the donors might have renewed
their hopes of a miracle, in spite of the murky sins they
more than likely suspected had denied them an answer to
their prayers, I would have flung the wretched plaques in
their faces. But the *tagari* had stuck to my side like a lung
infected with pleurisy.

Where would it end? My legs supported me, but I
turned and ran, *anywhere*, into a formlessness of time and space.

It is all the more surprising that I should find myself seated,
legs curled under me to make a cushion, surrounded by
perfect calm. Beside me is this open suitcase overflowing
with letters – old, damp, mouldy, yellow. My only reason
for distress is the absence of my precious *tagari*. I must have
dropped it as I ran. Good riddance to the metal tokens
with which it was stuffed. But I am now without the only
possession I valued, and which I could call my own.

'Heavens, what on earth is this?' Her voice sounds incre-
dulous as she kicks at the shabby Globeite.

'A suitcase, I imagine. No, I don't. It *is*.'

'But from where? It can't be from the garage. I've
checked the contents of every suitcase stored down there.
Anyway, you couldn't have opened the door. You haven't
the strength.'

'Who knows what the possessed possess?' I can't help
sniggering as I come up with my reply. 'And the garage
isn't the store-room of *all* our secrets. Large houses have
corners which even the professionally inquisitive haven't
explored.'

Her hand reaches down and stirs the contents of the
suitcase. 'All these – what are they?' The hand withdraws
as though bitten by a spider.

'Letters – can't you see? Perhaps also prayers. That's something you the rationalist wouldn't understand. If only I could find my *tagari* I might prove to you that prayers sometimes twitter in the metal voices of those who offer them.'

'You must hand over the suitcase. All these letters are my concern – as archivist.'

I can't disagree with her in words. I am too feeble after my flight from Nisos to this other, greater, in many ways more distressing island. I make a little gesture and stir the surface of yellowed letters, picking out a couple at random.

I read, and my voice trembles with released emotion, 'I will believe you love me if you reveal yourself. But you never do. Surely you can give me a clue, at some humble, earthly level?' And I open the second letter, more desperately because of the damp mould which seals the dart or aeroplane shape in which it is folded. ' . . . is it unnatural that I should ask you to strengthen my belief? Oh God, surely not? I am only human . . .'

Like the letter-paper, my voice sticks to itself: it can hardly separate the several sheets of meaning enfolding it. 'There, you see – a prayer – as I said. And I am very wrong in asking you to share feelings so private that revealing them becomes an enormity.'

She practically snatches the letters from me and throws them back amongst the freckled chaos in the suitcase.

'Don't upset yourself, Mother. You should let others interpret the past – objectively. That's why I've made a point of taking charge of any papers which concern the family.'

She snaps the hasps on the bulging Globeite. And that, Hilda believes, is that.

All around me the Park like a waking dream. Perhaps in time it will turn into a nightmare as Ayia Ekaterini did. But not for the moment. The ugly mynas stalk, squeak, and fly into the branches of the paperbacks. There is an old man with matted hair and a hand down his back, scratching. Probably a mystic.

'Come on, Mother.' She reaches down, offering to pull me to my feet. 'Your joints will set if you sit there for ever on this damp ground.'

'You don't realise how supple I've remained from being a dancer. And, I'm cushioned by my haunches against this – bog.'

I can tell from the vibrations that Hilda is becoming impatient. She says, moreover, 'I can't stay here arguing.'

'Admittedly, the thigh muscles of some dancers tighten so that, in the end, they can't give birth. They strangle the children they are trying to expel. Anyway, my dancer's thighs didn't prevent me expelling you and Hal.'

'Oh, come on! I'm expecting a telephone call.'

'Who on earth would ring Hilda?'

She doesn't answer. So I get up without distorting my body to any great extent, leaving a saucer in the ground. Looking back over my shoulder, I see the saucer filled with moisture.

'I hope it isn't blood.'

'What is?'

'That liquid in the hollow where I was sitting. There's an awful lot of blood about.'

'Nonsense. Come along at once.'

She speaks to me as though I am a little girl.

'I'm not ready. I have to limber up. You can't understand how important it is. You can't believe in my

85

connection with the dance. Ask your father – your grandfather – who were there when I performed in front of an
audience of celebrities in Washington DC.'

I execute an arabesque. The effort is pretty agonising.
Hilda refuses to look. She marches off, lugging the dismal
suitcase.

'If I take my clothes off, it could be easier and more
convincing.'

She turns round in horror. I have already unzipped as
far as my cleavage.

'Not in the Park!' she hisses.

'At this hour there's nobody here. Except the Mystic –
whose mind is on higher things. And that big black dog in
the distance.'

Hilda's poor little face crinkles. 'Oh, Mummy, you do
make me suffer.'

So I know I have the upper hand. 'The trouble with
ordinary people is they haven't suffered enough.'

We walk abreast. I take my little girl by the hand. I cry
with joy. We are both crying.

But Hilda stops. She is afraid she is making a fool of
herself, and that anyone coming across us might equate her
with her 'mad mother'.

'What they don't understand is that joy and suffering are
interchangeable.' I slow down the words rolling around in
my mouth, I listen for reaction. Am I losing control of my
Australian child?

'You must be ravenous, darling. I'll boil you an egg.'

'Bloody eggs!' I throw away her hand, 'Words are what
matter. Even when they don't communicate. That's why
I must continue writing. Somebody may understand in
time. All that I experienced on Nisos – as Cassianí – in any

of my lives, past or future – as Benedict, Magda, Dolly Formosa. Somebody', I look back, 'could understand to-morrow ... I don't aspire to God the Father – but one of his understudies – that mystic for instance ...'

This same character is still following us, with pauses to search through the contents of rubbish bins and to scratch his back.

'That's no mystic. He's a lousy old derro.' So speaks my uncharitable daughter.

'I ought to ask him home. He might have the answers.'

'Over my dead body! Lice added to the white ant and cockroaches.'

'To share the contents of each other's souls. While you rummage to your heart's content through a suitcase of mouldy archival letters.'

I look back again.

'And that big black dog. A dog is what I need.'

'He'll kill your cats.'

'My cats hate me. But this dog may be sent as atonement for the dog I murdered – Hilary's Danny. I can feel his tongue licking the sins from my sticky hands. All sin is sticky, don't you think? Blood, and semen, and condensed milk. I shall call him – why not? Dog.'

None of my plans mature the moment they are conceived. They have to be proved acceptable, pass through a novitiate so to speak.

Hilda/Hulda rings Patrick. Patrick comes, leaning on his stick, the born Mother Superior.

Hilda goes. 'My friend Mrs McDermott is expecting me.'

I have never discovered who this Mrs McDermott is, but

am happy Hilda is not friendless. I'm sure the McDermott is 'safe'. Probably Presbyterian – an *agnostic* Presbyterian.

When Hilda has left us Patrick and I enjoy a slight giggle. There is nothing in holy writ to say the pursuit of salvation hasn't its humorous side. Teresa herself when not in ecstasy was a jolly, bouncing girl.

Patrick is stalking about the room supported by his stick, wearing the invisible conventual veil, Puccini would have adored him.

I tell him I shall make some tea. 'And bread–and–butter rolls?'

Out of charity he declines the bread–and–butter rolls.

In the kitchen I am suddenly afraid. What am I embarking on? Is it ever safe to take a person into one's confidence? Even a friend of such long standing as Patrick. He and I have been so close we have lain in bed together, holding each other as the flying-foxes shriek in the Port Jackson figs, and at times enter the room, to hang upside down from the ceiling above us. As we lay together I wondered if any flicker of unseen eyelashes gave him cause to remember that he had been my husband's lover, or that I could translate myself at will into the form of my hated mother-in-law, in other words his ex-lover's mother. There was no sign, and the flying-foxes continued squeaking inside and outside the house.

But now in the kitchen I'm afraid. I scatter tea, you would think a mouse plague had broken out. I pour scalding water on my instep. How much has Hilda told Patrick? She can't know all that much. She couldn't conceive of life at Ayia Ekaterini. Could Patrick – the ersatz Reverend Mother patrolling the living room at the moment? Patrick himself is in search of the unanswerable, the unattainable.

He will know that we, the explorers, stop at nothing. He may smell on my body the semen of that crafty monk Onouphrios, or see me as Benedict leading the frail Bernadette deeper and deeper into the bush till in her fear and confusion she reveals to her strapping companion the source of goodness. All this is to come, of course. The worthy Patrick cannot possibly know that as Dolly Formosa I am prepared to tour every Australian outback town, devour however many sponges and Pavlovas in however many bourgeois lounge rooms after the nightly performance, in hopes of biting on a clue buried along with the passion-fruit seeds and the toothache at the heart of the cake.

My range is immense. There is no reason why I should doubt my potentialities. Yet here I dither in the kitchen instead of taking the tray and going out to the living room where Patrick is waiting. If only I could nip upstairs first and read all I have written about Alex Xenophon Demirjian Gray, past, present, and future.

To confirm that I am I.

I

If I were a certain kind of mousy little thing I would embroider that most important pronoun on a guest towel and hang it on a rail in the cloakroom.

But I am not.

Come on, Suor Angelica.

I click my heels like a Sarge. Seize the tray and march out to where I am expected by somebody who ought to know me as well as his own heartbeat, but doesn't – for better or worse.

Patrick has thrown off the Puccini persona. He is seated in an armchair, the walking stick slanted beside him. He is stroking his upper lip like a man.

He makes a grunting, heaving motion, as though to rise, while hoping he will be absolved through age, arthritis, and having known me, anyway outwardly, always.

'Don't! Don't!' the practised hostess pleads. 'I don't know how to apologise – for taking so long – to make a simple cup of tea.'

I settle the tray.

'Hilda takes care of this sort of thing. Usually.' I listen for the crash from a tipped tray. It doesn't occur.

'But if I'd persuaded her to stay and do the necessary, we shouldn't enjoy our privacy, should we?'

What a twit I am at times. And Patrick a clod. A bore this afternoon. Or am *I* the bore boring Patrick?

I seat myself after giving him his tea. 'Jasmine!' I remember to cross my ankles as I have seen the experts do. (What the hell, aren't I an expert?)

'Since when did you decide, Patrick, to grow a moustache?'

'Did I?'

'Don't I see you stroking a moustache?'

'A mannerism – a *tic*.'

We sit. I am convinced I saw the moustache. Could have been a shadow. Or something he abandoned with the Reverend Mother persona.

And now, we sit.

One of the most distressing situations is when two people who know each other by heart feel a gap widening between them, elastically, elastically, for no accountable reason. It is filling the room between myself and Patrick. We daren't look at each other. I can hear it twanging. In my mind innumerable stopgaps offer themselves, like a nest of seething maggots. None of them is desirable. I can feel myself growing more foolish by the second. If I open my mouth to speak I know that my teeth will show up long and yellow like those of an elderly ewe. If, for some reason, I were to bite Patrick he might turn septic.

Sheep haven't the wisdom of goats. For the moment I am completely lacking in wisdom.

I clear my throat finally. I cough it up like a gobbet of phlegm.

'Did Hilda tell you about the man we saw in the Park?' He looks alarmed. 'A man, Alex? What kind of man?'

'I'd say a mystic.' I hurry on to avoid what might become difficult. 'Hilda dismisses this person because she suspects him of lice. When he's probably only suffering from psoriasis. You know, the hand down the back.'

I hold up my own hand like a traffic cop. I am not yet ready to face advice or opinions. 'Hilda would be against anyone who promised illumination of any kind, and she would try to force her own adverse opinion on one. I have to form opinions for myself. Like relationships with human beings – or others – with *God* for that matter.'

Patrick might be suffering from wind, or his arthritis is tormenting his buttocks.

'So I've got this plan for cultivating the Mystic from the Park.'

I like the tone of my voice, it is mellow, dark as molasses. But Patrick might have been stupefied by Valium.

So I try another tack.

'Did she tell you about the letters I found? An old suitcase full of mouldy letters in a corner of the house she'd never explored.'

'No-oh . . .'

'Well, there are the letters. She grabbed them, needless

to say, but won't be able to interpret them, even if she succeeds in prising the damp sheets apart, because I suspect, from the couple I have read, that they are poems – or prayers – far beyond the archivist's comprehension. Shopping and laundry lists are more in her line. Wouldn't you agree?'

I shan't give him the chance, because today Patrick is not at his best.

'Well, I found the suitcase in what I call the priest hole. You know the secret room where the faithful used to hide their pet priest from the Prots. Hilda doesn't know we have such a refuge in our house. Hers is the pantry, amongst the pulses and detergents. Or the locked filing cabinets where she keeps her archives. Well, we have our priest hole. Which is where I found this grotty old suitcase full of poems – love-letters – prayers – whatever you like to call them. You approach it through the built-in cupboard in my bedroom. Inside, there is a second door, uncomfortably narrow, leading to this hideaway under the eaves. I might show you if . . .'

Patrick looks guilty, distraught, disbelieving, or perhaps only fearing the arthritic twinges the narrow door will bring on as he squeezes through.

'On second thoughts,' I decide, 'it may be wiser not to show you. It would put you at risk if I have to hide someone – not necessarily a priest – but a guerrilla during the invasion, or a revolutionary after concerned people have been forced to rise up against the Government. Anyhow, this is where I propose to keep the Mystic – safe from Hilda – when I've smuggled him in from the Park.'

I pause and take a good look at Patrick to see whether he is really on my side.

He says, and it sounds horribly like his on-and-off ally Hilda, 'I wouldn't advise you to smuggle him, Alex. Better bring him in openly, find out all about each other, on the ground floor. He might not live up to your expectations of illumination. Lightning flashes are less impressive in the living room, fireballs are extinguishable. Upstairs, the Mystic might crawl out of the cupboard, lice and all, and into your bed. An endless source of irritation.'

Patrick was always pompous. I set my face in the expression I know from many mirrors turns it into a stone wall. I don't know why I have ever persuaded myself to accept this old sod as my friend.

'During my life I've experienced, over and over, lice in the bed. Husbands and lovers included.'

I don't include 'friends', because Patrick, for all his sophistication, is too innocent to hurt.

As for the Mystic, I shall investigate him at some appropriate moment.

Patrick's mouth may be wrestling with that useful but non-committal word, so dear to English evaders, 'Quite'.

I hurry on. 'Did she tell you about the dog?'

'I don't think so. *No.*' He lurches forward in the chair as though propelled by a hiccup.

'The dog! The dog!' I hear myself shouting, reverberating. 'It's a wonder either of you missed out on that big black dog – must be a dumpling – who haunts the Park. Dogs have played such a part in our lives. Well, I mean to *adopt* this dog to atone for what I did to Hilary's Danny. I shall bring him in. He's called Dog. What else? There won't be any question of a priest hole for a dog. Not like the Mystic. Mystics can be contained – anyway, when off duty. A dog never. Hilda must learn to put up with him.

She put up with Danny, at least till I shot him, when she used his corpse to show up her father's wife as the big disaster of her life. So ...'

Again I was brought up short by a rush of mucus to my throat. I remembered the French mystic demonstrating her piety and self-abnegation by picking up from the street a gobbet of beggar's spittle and forcing herself to swallow it. Could I come at swallowing my Mystic's spittle if I managed to assemble Patrick and Hilda at the same time to witness my self-mortification and acknowledge my sanctity?

Or would the big, black, bounding Dog save me by forestalling the act?

'Dog has many purposes,' I tell my audience of one.

He replies, 'I think you are over-excited, Alex, and I must catch my bus.'

Fortunately for him, Hilda returns at just this moment. 'Have you enjoyed your talk?' she asks, smiling that little watery smile which masquerades as sincerity in a dutiful daughter.

As Patrick is in a hurry they go out together into the porch.

She comes back so quickly they can't have had time to collaborate against their schizophrenic's mystic and dog.

I continue sitting by the tray because I am too apathetic to move from the position, or the role Patrick at his deadliest had forced me to play. I imagine him on the bus, trying to impress his neighbour (provided he is personable) before reaching his destination. I forget where Patrick lives today with that growing stack of foolscap which he hopes will bring him fulfilment.

Hilda is starting to fuss – the tray, the slops. If she knew how to produce one, she would offer me a baked custard *tout de suite*, and hustle Mummy off to bed.

But tonight I am not to be hustled. I sit on in the contracting light planning a future dominated by the Mystic and Dog.

'Are you all right, Mummy?' Hilda calls from the distance.

Little does she know.

'I am OK,' I call back in the vernacular, to irritate us both.

I intended to act immediately, but Patrick must have got into me. I debate endlessly with myself in deciding which time of day or night to carry out my plan. Crims and missionaries and little old ladies would go ahead in broad daylight. Schizophrenics and fellow mystics would no doubt favour the hours of darkness. Should I consider Hilda's whereabouts – and those others who haunt our house? The telephone could ring (Patrick out of malice) alerting Hilda before I can muffle the call. Then I am held up by the minor considerations of dress and make-up. Should I wear white to convey my bona fides to the Mystic? When Dog would surely destroy the effect by dragging muddy paws from waist to hemline. Eyeliner and a touch of shadow might bring the Mystic on, but alarm a dog into barking its head off.

So I had, and still have what the radio calls 'problems'. Anxiety creases a whole wardrobe of pretty and foolish frocks, and makes me break out in perspiration at the armpits. (Snuffle, snuffle, Dog might appreciate the sweat.)

Several times I have been to the Park searching for the objects of what has become an obsession. I have not yet been rewarded. Once I thought I saw the Mystic in the distance, and hurried panting towards this figure, scattering a flock of galahs feasting on a patch of nutgrass, only to find a disgusting derro rummaging through an overflow of week-end garbage. He shouted at me, I could not hear what. I retreated, and on returning home, found shoes scuffed by drought-ravaged earth, shoulders blistered by summer heat. Once in the night a huge black bird slid towards me across the waters of the lake beside which I was walking, and at the same time a flasher accosted me from under a paperback. At such moments I would like my little girl to take me by the hand, but as I have been aware for years, Hilda is never around when needed.

I don't know whether to feel relieved or resentful when I hear my latch-key crunching in the lock. Would I get my own back on H. if she ever finds my brains littering the porch? I very much doubt it. Much as she detests the look and smell of brains.

In my writing-book I write cross out write cross out again again can I believe that I AM I I must find the Mystic I must find DOG his big spatulate slavering tongue which may obliterate and redeem

end of passage

It is a Friday when I come across the Mystic. I don't know where Hilda has gone – to Mrs McDermott her agnostic friend? to deliver a bundle of clothes to Lifeline, which not even the desperate destitute would mould to their existential bodies – or to buy a packet of dried apricots or split peas? Anyway, on leaving the house, I cannot sense Hilda's presence above the ticking of clocks and white ant.

And there he is, only a stone's throw from the house which is ours, and which I intend to offer him as his, if he will obey certain desirable rules. The Mystic is picking through the overspill of garbage left by human beings from their week-end picnics, beside the lake, with its scum of plastic, corpses of ducks, and live, vengeful swans.

We study each other.

I am wearing a little pleated knee-length frock in pale grey which should do justice to the Mystic, and on which the marks of Dog's paws will not be so noticeable should he turn up.

Over lips which are pale, but fleshy, the Mystic calls, 'Waddayerknow, I found a whole tin uv opened bully, not a maggot in it.'

I reply, 'Can you be absolutely sure? I'd say there's a maggot lurking anywhere – even in the best-intentioned Fray Bentos or Swift's.'

We look at each other, can I believe with understanding?

He laughs. 'You got something there – lady.'

'I am not a lady. I am Alexandra Xenophon Demirjian Gray of anywhere you like to name.'

After a pause he delivers a message, over those pale but fleshy lips, 'I'll buy that. You can call me Joe.'

Joe Jojo Joyo I am overjoyed it is the first time someone has confirmed that life can exist for the condemned.

We laugh together. It doesn't matter that his teeth are rotten brown stumps. I take him by what many would see as his repulsive hand. I hope I'm not wearing too many rings. I only wear all this Byzantine clobber because thieves may break in while I am abroad. Fortunately he doesn't seem to notice. It makes me ashamed of the shudder which ran through my body on first taking hold of fingers as stiff as a turtle's neck, every wrinkle ingrained with black. Madame Guyon would have approved of my mystic. She would have lapped him up. Unlike myself, Madame G. was experienced in all the techniques of piety.

(A strange admission: I could never admit to a friend, let alone my writing-books, that I am an amateur in any sphere of art, life, or spiritual practice. Alas, it seems I am a hypocrite – perhaps at this early stage only half of one. Hand in hand with Joe I shall persevere.)

Just as he doesn't seem to notice the Byzantine rings Grandfather Gray looted from the Middle East, and which I am wearing on every finger, I would say he is unimpressed by the house – by most standards an 'important' one – to which I have brought him. Perhaps he is distracted by the itch. As I lead him across the threshold he sticks a hand down his back and starts scratching with a frenzy greater than psoriasis or the lice diagnosed by Hilda demands. He scratches and scratches. I almost shed tact and ask what is wrong, but luckily, am guided in a safer direction by an unseen power.

'Can't I bring you anything to eat?' I ask.

He sighs before replying, 'Thanks, but I done pretty well outer the garbage in the last few days. It's always that much tastier when a bloke's gotter fossick for it.'

Again the hypocrite, I agree. (Oh dear am I perhaps not a half but a whole?)

'What I'd like more than anythun is ter rest me carcase for a bit before I take off on the next lap.'

Without waiting for permission he flops down on a sofa in what we have been calling the living room. I am racked by a dread that Hilda might return and see him there, if she isn't already spying on us through a peephole known only to herself.

I come out with appropriate noises, from which emerges the suggestion, 'Surely you won't be leaving us so soon? I was hoping you might think of making this your home. As far as one has a home, of course, in the lives we lead.'

He seemed to be pondering over what I had said, then actually hawked up some phlegm on Hilda's cherished Afghan rug.

'That's spot-on!' he said. 'You're lucky if they let you in again at sundown – not enough beds with the population explodun' every minute.'

I never consider myself spot-on. I'm happy if I'm anywhere near the target. In fact I was thinking how can I deal with this phlegm on the Afghan. Madame Guyon would not have hesitated.

I am nerving myself when Hilda comes in and discovers me on all fours.

'What on earth . . . ? Mother!'

'I've been wondering whether the moth . . .'

'You know I make a point of spraying regularly. Get up at once. It's not a position for old joints to get locked in.'

Mercifully the Mystic seems to have vanished.

She helps me up in spite of my attempts to shake her off. 'You forget how supple I am after years of yoga and dancing. They're what have kept me mentally and physically in tune.'

She draws in her chin in such a way I can tell she has been with her Scottish friend the Presbyterian agnostic. Sure enough, she starts telling me a long and totally uninteresting story about Mrs McD. and a cairngorm she found years ago in the Cairngorm Mountains on an expedition organised by a gemstone society she belonged to.

'You've never told me your friend's *Christian* name. Names give a clue to character.'

'We've never been on first-name terms,' Hilda replies quite primly. 'Anyway, she found her cairngorm. She wears it today in a silver brooch surrounded by coloured pebbles. She was led, she is convinced, to the spot where the gem was hidden, and broke open the rock with the little hammer she always carried in her haversack.'

'If Brenda was *led* to the cairngorm, I can't believe she's an agnostic.'

'How do you know she's a Brenda?'

'She sounds like one. And she's not a silly old agnostic. She can only be a mystic.'

'I'm not going to have a religious argument, Mother, at this time of day.'

She is stalking towards the kitchen as virtuously as her friend. Her back is pure Brenda McDermott.

I do what I can to pacify my Hilda. 'I'd give anything to see her old cairngorm.'

'She lost it once, and it turned up in the oatmeal barrel.'

'There, you see, not only a mystic, but an alcoholic as well.'

Hilda is too offended to answer.

I go off at a tangent. 'Did you see anyone hanging round on your way in?'

'Nobody.'

'There wasn't a man – a rather hairy one?'

'No man – neither hairy not smooth.'

In some ways a relief, though it could mean the Mystic had hidden somewhere in the house without being shown where the refuge is. He could pounce out on Hilda from a dark corner and give her the fright of her life.

'Or a dog, Hilda? You didn't see a big black mongrel dog?'

'A dog – yes – lifting his leg in the garden, killing the plants. I chased him back into the Park before he did too much damage.'

'O-o-hh! But he's mine. That's Dog!'

'You know you never liked dogs, Mother. If you did you wouldn't have shot Danny with Father's revolver.'

'Oh, yes, I know I committed a murder. In fact I've committed several. I imagine it's impossible to get through life without. And now – but you wouldn't understand. Dog has been sent to atone for the evil I was born with – to lick me clean.'

As she rounds on me, I see Hilda at her sourest, 'If the brute is so dedicated, no doubt he'll turn up again and do his duty.'

Between the vanished Mystic and the runaway Dog, I am torn in opposite directions. I feel the screams start to mount inside me, till I catch sight of Professor Falkenberg holding out the seamless canvas jacket, its blind sleeves, its dangling tapes.

'I will be good!' I choke on my sobs, and quieten down.

It must have convinced Hilda because she has left me to my own pursuits.

What to do, though? I am too agitated to start recording the events of the day.

From the pantry I can hear her putting things away. Putting away is one of her favourite pastimes.

I suppose I could go upstairs and put away my rings – except I can feel that the rings, too, have forsaken me – all but the wedding ring which fits too tightly. More than once I thought of having it sawn off. Then I decided it would come in handy during chapters of my convent life.

I am alone in this house with a ring which has eaten into my flesh. More grace is shown to the birds of Heaven, flirting in the garden in their hundreds – finches, wrens, honey-eaters, bulbuls – tossing the spray from the sprinklers out of their feathers as they cleave the fern-fronds. If a bird flew into the room I might hold its rejuvenating form between my withered breasts . . .

No bird offers itself.

I am on my way upstairs. I hear a noise. It can only be a male. When a husband or lover has the upper hand over wife or mistress whose sensibility he no longer respects, he farts in her presence. I believe I recognise this sound.

On the half-landing I am seized by the wrist, by a steely, yet clammy, male hand. The force of obsession brings us close together, breast to breast, mouth to mouth. I am pervaded by the stench of cabbage, halitosis, and metho.

A voice whines, 'What'uv yer brought me 'ere for? Waddayer expect a bloke ter do?'

I realise it is the Mystic with whom I am mouth to mouth in the dark, and that he is the one in need of resuscitation when I had expected so much of him.

'Steady on!' I burble into the brown cavern of his mouth in what I hear as the voice of my father-in-law Henry Gray ordering a shickered friend to get a hold on himself.

It would have seemed a situation exclusively involving Edwardian, middle-aged males, one of them superior to the other through investments and class, if I hadn't suddenly felt so lithe and youthful inside my snug-fitting made-to-measure suit. As for my partner, he was losing that bagginess of the park derro, and on a different level, the hairy image of the desert father, prophet, mystic I had hoped to instruct me in arcane knowledge.

Ambi-sex explains itself as my little glacé boots patter down the long curve of stairway towards the stage prepared for our performance. I hear, not far behind me, my partner's soft-shoe slapdash. Sound and purpose are practically delirious as we reach the floor and whirl out across its black glass surface. My head beneath the little topper is bursting with song, which the daringly painted lips release. I strut and capriole, '*Bert, Bert, I haven't a shirt ...*' the picture of exultant vanity, tossing the monocle skywards at the end of its moiré ribbon, then catching the frame in the socket of my knowing eye.

As for my partner, he is not yet resentful of partnership, he does his stuff meticulously, his own topper reflecting mine, as he soft-shoes around in his grey spats, a shadow to my substance. I look back lovingly, not to say longingly, to encourage his somewhat superfluous part in our act. Jojo is no Fred, but he has done his best to slick down his hair with brilliantine, his moustache no broader than an eyebrow. Nothing much can be done about the wrists, they are – well, hairy. What odds, girls? Doesn't skin respond to the tingle of hair against skin? *As we stroll down the Strand – at ten-thirty – every manjack Burlington Bertie from Bow ...*

Oh my God, Ella! Joe's had it. Arches falling. It's too long a trail. Sawdust underfoot by now, these six guys pounding out a grey number on the white-and-gold mini-pianos, '*... Bert, Bert, I haven't a shirt .... as I stroll down the Strand ... gloves in my hand ...*' No clap tonight for Little

Ella Old Hat! Have to try out another on 'em. '*We're going back back back to Yarrawonga . . .*' A burnt-out case before we're into it.

'Yeah, I'm tired,' I tell the mike, 'what I'm really looking forward to is opening a family cocktail lounge back home in Melbourne. Enjoy a quiet Manhattan. Joe here will bear me out . . .' Lead him forward – make it look warm – except here's this goddam wedding ring! And the wig is lobotomising my aspirinated skull. Joe my joyous husband looks less than enthusiastic as the kids and grandkids line up behind us for the family show in St Kilda.

'What 'uv yer brought me 'ere for? Waddaya expect a bloke ter do?'

Some something some act is finished.

We are standing confronting each other on my bedroom floor. We might never have gone through the dance routine in which the glass surface becomes the sawdust trail of ordinary life.

But haven't I set out to rise above ordinariness? Isn't this why I brought in my personal Mystic from the Park?

'Listen,' I appeal desperately, 'you've got so much to tell me, but the time isn't ripe for us to settle down to what I think the radio calls a seminar. Right? For one thing, my earthly daughter might come in. So I've got to keep you for what I see as the auspicious moment. In the meantime I can hide you safely. I shan't say all that comfortably, but mystics, desert fathers, prophets, have never expected comfort, have they? In fact, they've gone out of their way to avoid it. So – I'll hide you in the priest hole . . .'

'Eh?' he burps in my face.

'You'll be fed – modestly. Those of our belief don't ask for more.'

I rummage in my handkerchief drawer and bring out the tin of bully with every word of the Fray Bentos gospel printed on the label. 'See – darling? And if you cut your hands opening the tin you can remember Christ bleeding on the Cross.'

He is too bemused to murmur more than, 'Oke.'

'And now the priest hole ...' I open the door of the built-in cupboard (the door through which the pest inspector squeezes once a year, unwillingly if he is a stout person) and push the Mystic past the racks of dresses dangling listless till animated by my body, each one a ghost of past perfumes and performances, into the hideous space that smells of damp and possum.

'Careful,' I warn. 'If your feet don't balance on the joists, you may go through the lath and find yourself in the presence of HILDA the frustrated saint.'

'Rely on me,' mutters the Mystic, clutching the tin of Fray Bentos as his mainstay.

I am so relieved as I slam the door to find myself alone.

Isn't this perhaps what I've always wanted from away back? No husbands lovers fathers children saints mystics. Only when you're stranded amongst the human furniture, the awfulness of life, you've got to set out on a search to find some reason for it all.

But now the great worrier starts worrying again. What if I bolted the door to the priest hole on the wardrobe side? And forget or don't want to remember – will a mummified corpse be found, smelling of a mystic's metho instead of the traditional eucalyptic piss of the entombed possum?

I climb into bed. I am *determined* not to think. But nobody can protect us from the reality of dreams. I hear a dog, no ordinary one, but Dog, baying at the three-cornered moon. I go downstairs, made dizzy by the branches of the paperbarks. A wind is let loose around me, a warm moist wind ballooning the skirt of my nightie round the varicose veins I have always hoped to hide.

Dog has returned from the Park. He is waiting outside the glass doors, on the tiled veranda. His yellow eyes. His yellow fangs bared in a kindly, doggish grin, if they didn't suggest the bars of a prison from which I've always been hoping to escape.

I let him in.

'Good dog,' I encourage, I kiss one of my many saviours. 'Remember that what I did to Danny was done while I was of unsound mind. Professor Falkenberg will tell you that.'

But the dog appears not to have heard me. He starts scampering upstairs, admittedly on felted pads, but with a devil's thumping which shakes the whole house. He must have been here before.

I start after the infernal beast. What if Hilda . . . ? What if the Mystic . . . ?

Oh, Dog! Oh, God!

He has landed on my bed, and lies there in the lion couchant position, fringed paws outstretched, the purple tongue waiting to savour the salt of human flesh, or do his *real* job of absolving sin.

From the priest hole a rattling of the bolted door leading to the wardrobe. A frail bolt to anyone endowed with average strength, let alone supernatural gifts. Across the landing, Hilda turning in her dreams.

Dare I get on the bed with Dog? He glares and stares. Waiting.

I pray with all the violence I am capable of injecting

into my prayers. I pray to be removed to another situation. And as usually happens, my prayer is answered. (If I keep up this sort of thing I may qualify as a candidate for canonisation. I may even pass the Test and contribute something to the Australian tourist industry by becoming Centennial Park's Very Own Saint.)

Twigs break and crackle under our boots. Some of the older, more nervous Sisters hope it is not the crackle of fire. It has been one of those summers when natural outlines are blurred by smoke or mist. It is often difficult to decide which, unless by a change of temperature. The weather is unpredictable: one minute the black cockatoos screaming as they are pursued by flames, the next rejoicing in the white mists, the natural element of gang gangs, which seep through the gullies and swirl about the heights.

'I love to hear the gang gangs,' I remark to Bernadette when conversation is running short.

'Gang gangs?' in her old tremulous voice.

'The black cockatoos. I'll show you in the bird book in Sister Barbara's libr'y.'

Bernadette exists above the habits, the language of birds. She has this disbelieving smile. In spite of my love for her, there are times when her sanctity gets me down. Now I have to take hold of myself, as I guide her by an arm fragile as a wishbone, through bush blurred by smoke or mist. Around and ahead of us nuns are calling, squawking at one another, in fear of their surroundings – or for pleasure at their escape from routine.

Reverend Mother has ordained the picnic for the Friday before Epiphany. In spite of the obvious advantages, I know she already regrets her daring, but a sense of her own authority will never let her down. Her voice twitters through the scrub at her party of nuns and schoolgirls. Most of the boarders are away at their homes, only those who live at a distance remain in our care during the Christmas holidays. Some of these girls, Narelle for instance, and Philomena, have excused themselves from the Epiphany picnic, claiming they are unwell. One or two of the less dedicated nuns, hinting at a period, are also absent.

Despite her authority, Reverend Mother sounds jittery as she hustles her white cockatoos through the bush. She picks on the sumpter mules, Finbarr and slave labour from the kitchen laden with the wherewithal for this picnic. Here Reverend Mother can congratulate herself on her miraculous idea, the Feast of Kippers. What more appropriate and modest than a raw kipper on the Friday before Epiphany? The father of one of her girls, an export-import agent, developer, shipowner, engaged in other less mentionable – but even more profitable pursuits, has unloaded this cargo of kippers on our House. God-sent in Reverend Mother's book. The smell of sweating, smoked kipper should be whetting our appetites as we tramp in disarray towards some destination still to be revealed to Reverend Mother.

I hope I am not cynical. 'Have you ever chewed on a raw kipper?' I ask Bernadette.

'A what?'

No matter. We drop the subject.

I look towards Finbarr weighed down with baskets and carrier bags more heavily than any of her slave assistants.

I should offer to help, but know that I am jealous of Finbarr, of her strong, freckled hands caked with bran and pollard, her smell of the piglets and poultry she tends. She is both strong and indispensable. Benedict longs to challenge her strength and indispensability. But since I am in charge of Bernadette, the oldest, frailest member of our Order, I can only cast regrettable glances of jealousy and dislike at the stalwart Finbarr – almost a man in her nun's habit.

Pooh!

Somewhere around the appropriate hour a suitable clearing reveals itself to Reverend Mother for the Feast of Kippers. Finbarr and the sumpter mules shed their panniers on the meagre, scrub grass. Some of the less dutiful Sisters and more exhausted schoolgirls plump down without further ado. Bernadette's old light-weight, music-hall boots only skim the ground supported as she is by Benedict. Her smile suggests she is enjoying her gratuitous levitation. I settle her on a bed of grey, fallen leaves, her ancient back propped against the butt of a giant redgum. She plays automatically with her girdle of beads, while Benedict is free to take part in other, more material activities.

It is soon clear that Benedict's dislike of the full-time farm hand is reciprocated by Finbarr. As I unload the contents of basket and carrier bag, the freckled hands are constantly interfering, the coarse voice muttering disapproval. Crockery and food are re-arranged from where I have laid them. 'Not there, Sister. Here, as Reverend Mother would expect.' I am almost asphyxiated by Finbarr's *red* smell, disgusted by farmyard pollard encrusting the Bride's ring.

Envious, too. The ring I wear has fulfilled too many purposes. Finbarr, not Benedict, is the true Bride of Christ.

Everything goes more or less according to Reverend

Mother's plan. Grace is said. Bread is broken. We appear to enjoy our ginger-beer – too gaseous for some of us. Lips express largely unconvincing appreciation as we mumble fragments of sweated kipper. There is for each a runtish, worm-eaten apple from the tree in Finbarr's garden.

Benedict sits beside Bernadette holding to the old nun's lips a cup of tepid ginger-beer. The old thing's age, her humility, and gratitude, suggest she is partaking of a sacrament.

What to do about the Kipper? Shall I masticate a few shreds and feed it between the lips of this elderly, helpless fledgling? She will accept it as another sign of grace.

Reverend Mother is frowning, jittering worse than ever as she glances skywards. I am always fascinated by the little black hairy mole at the entrance to her left nostril. Now it is almost jumping off her skin like some demented insect. As she claps her hands. As she directs directionlessly. 'Sister Finbarr, we must hurry, please.' It is anybody's guess whether the white to greyish skeins tangling with the upper reaches of the trees, are smoke, mist or a judgment. The world as we know it is temporarily obscured. 'Sisters – all you girls – Mary, Angela, Josephine, Diana – lend Sister Finbarr a hand.'

Chaos on the droughty, scrub grass. Josephine has broken a cup.

'Benedict,' no longer 'Sister', it could not have been more pointed. 'You are in charge of Sister Bernadette.'

You're telling me! I can be common when I choose, especially amongst this gaggle of crummy suburban nuns and new-rich schoolgirls. I stare back long and fiercely at the demented black hairy mole performing its antics at the base of Reverend Mother's left nostril.

We are more or less organised at last. We have our marching orders. We move off, except for the broken cup, fragments of born-stale bread, and the skins and backbones of tainted kipper.

Sisters Bernadette and Benedict are somewhat removed from the main body of the army. A wing of our own. Are we covering a retreat, or preparing to fight battles the Lord prepares for those he will receive into his bosom as well as those he plans to reject?

By now Bernadette's little-bird's cheep can scarcely be heard. 'Hold hard, Sister. My bunion is givun me gyp.'

'No reason, dear, why we shouldn't rest a little.' Just as if we were sisters of the everyday world.

As the cries of the cohorts recede, we sink down on a bed of leaves.

'That's right, Sister. Say a rosary or two ...'

In the whirling grey, of leaves, mist, smoke and gusts of doubt to which we who have surrendered the will to decide are prone.

Early light has strewn the twitched sheets of my bed with a pearly grey opalescence, gentle enough in tone if it did not also convey grey bodies almost strangled by their dreams. I am still wearing my grey frock. I am not lying on my bed, which is almost fully occupied by Dog.

'Dog, darling, do get down,' I hear myself whimper. 'Let me take you back to the Park. Don't you feel we were both mistaken?'

Obviously Dog still has to make up his mind. He lays his muzzle on his front paws, the yellow eyes investigating a situation he can only half believe in. Even Dog has his beliefs, and I am not, I never have been, one of them.

I hear Hilda moan from across the landing, 'Oh God, can't you let me off the hook? I never – never asked – to be born to any of it ...'

Dog growls back huffily.

Then I begin to hear this distraught jiggling from beyond the wardrobe, from inside the priest hole, as its prisoner struggles to burst the bolt on the connecting door.

What shall I do? If only I had the authority of Reverend Mother, tic and all, the sanctity of Sister Bernadette. Instead, I am I.

O God ...

I hear the bolt give. I've got to accept it. I fling open the wardrobe door. The Mystic plunges head first through the racks of – let's face it – musty dresses. He is bleeding at the mouth. He is clutching the half-opened tin of Fray Bentos bully.

'The key they give yer with the tin don't work,' he bellows. 'Bring a bloke a bloody can-opener.'

His tongue is protruding like a bull's pizzle.

'Plenty of good meat if only yer could get at it.'

Smelling blood and meat, Dog almost barks his head off, making little scampering thigh movements on the bed.

'Listen,' I tell my deranged Mystic. 'You should know the difference between meat and flesh. You should know when your faith is being tried by your reactions to Our Lord bleeding on the Cross – and what the Holy Spirit expects of us believers.'

The Mystic only looks mystified, as though the metho is still stirring in his blood.

'You're the one,' I begin to scream, 'the one I expected guidance from – when now it seems I must guide *you* –

you and this poor misguided, mongrel of a dog – back into the Park where you belong, along with the garbage, the plastic, and the flashers.'

'Never went much on dawgs,' he complains, then after a pause, in which several drops of blood drop from his human tongue to the floor-boards, 'any'ow, I'll take me bully with me.'

'Come,' I order them, and it could have been Reverend Mother in the flush of her calculated authority, 'I don't doubt you'll find your way. You have the double benefit of moon and daylight.'

Burping, panting, stumbling, padding, my pair of scrapped idols follow me down the path. The gate squeaks. I offer them the freedom of the street, where they vanish, perhaps gratefully.

As those who have failed to make it are grateful for small mercies.

As I am grateful for the bed of leaves on which I have experienced a sort of rest holding a prospective saint in my arms after the Feast of Kippers the Friday before Epiphany.

I shall remember the night Bernadette and Benedict were lost in the bush as the most peaceful I ever spent. Spiritually peaceful I mean, because of course there have been, blissful, invalid episodes after a plate of *trahaná* or *galatoboúriko*, and barely conscious memories of the breasts of my sweet Smyrna *nounoú*.

Bernadette and Benedict settle and re-settle together like two birds in the cold of morning in the nest we have rounded out at the foot of the giant redgum. What is so delicious about the situation is that we have temporarily abandoned those concepts of vocation, of sanctity, of aspiring to fulfil the wishes of the Holy Spirit. We are two birds suffering from goose-flesh, in fear of being plucked by the Almighty Poulterer if he doesn't overlook us in the mist – or smoke-ridden dawn light.

Bernadette and Benedict, sisters in a lost world. Reduced to this common sisterhood, I am not the one who could tell my adored Bernadette the story of my true life. Yet Bernadette, through inherent innocence and truthfulness, offers the documentary of hers.

'I was born, dear, the middle one in a family of seven, to parents from Galway and Glasgow. Me mother ran a little corner shop in Woolloomooloo, me dad was lost to the grog and the racecourse. Father ... I forget ... Damien Xavier ... ?'

'So be it, darling. I expect it was Father Damien Xavier.'

'That's right, dear. You got it. Father D.X. saw me as the salvation of me family. More than the family, it seemed, after he had taken a glass above what he ought!'

We, the sisters, snuggled deeper to warm the leaves we depended on this night in the bush.

'It was easy for me, I tell you, dear, not to commit a sin – see? 'Cos that was the way I was born. Only once I committed one.'

Painfully Bernadette munched on a mouthful of old teeth.

'What was this sin, my darling?' I clasp her tighter to my breasts, they have become all ears now that we are promised revelations for the Sunday morning press.

'I stole, Benedict, a pinch of jellybeans from a jar in me mother's shop.'

'Poor darling, I bet they tasted good.'

'No, dear. They didn't.'

Her old teeth are wheezing in the frosty dawn.

'Then I absolve you, darling – if Father X.D. or whatever, and the Lord Himself, don't. I absolve you from the
sin which wasn't.'

She sighs feebly. She isn't dying, surely, in my arms? Or
is it that she knows she was born above sin and jellybeans
– in other words, she was earmarked for beatification long
before Pope Thingummy decided Australia should have a
Saint.

I kiss her, I hug her, as a sister of this world. Her old
body makes faint fluttering bird sounds and motions. Oh
God, is she departing this life? Is Benedict strong enough to
cope with an ascension? My own body is unbelievably
strong and helpless.

Dawn, from insinuating, is mercilessly streaming like a
whole orchestra of alarm clocks. Only, my dear little Bernadette seems unaware. Currawongs, crows, kookaburras,
magpies, the lot, have begun shouting at anyone deaf
enough not to hear. Finally, most dreadful, human voices.

I shake my little cotton-filigree bird, my rag doll, crying,
'Wake up! Wake up! They'll be on us – the rescue party
– before you can say knife . . .'

She barely lifts her tired little, wrinkled, bird's eyelids.

If a Popemobile arrives with the rescue party, I see that
the intermediate stages will be skipped, and our Bernadette
elevated to the same level as every Thérèse in the calendar.
All hail to Mum and her corner shop, Dad the racecourse
tout, and Father X.D. (or D.X.) for his hard work after
the second glass.

As for me, Benedict is the only one consigned to deso-
lation, for love of my pure little unattainable darling. I am
not fit to swing on the hem of her skirt as she shoots like

a muslin rocket skywards. I shall remain I – Empress Alexandra of Byzantium Nicaea Smyrna Benha and Sydney Australia.

O God have mercy on all turds, whether dropped by elephants, goats or humans – Ameen.

Men are arriving on the scene in boots stouter than nuns wear. Gorgeous brutes in blue shirts and clone moustaches. They massacre a couple of saplings and improvise a stretcher by uniting them with a great-coat.

'OK, love – sorry – Sister!'

They lay my little scrap of divine love and failing flesh on their lopsided stretcher.

They are so pleased with themselves it is touching. (They must go to early mass.) Benedict they ignore. They can never ever have been to the Australian Opera, or they would have seen a drag version of a nun.

We start off.

The stretcher pitches alarmingly as they tramp over rock, through wiry tussock. Their precious burden may shoot off if they don't take care. She would rise above it, of course. To Saint Bernadette no worse than landing on a bed of angels' feathers.

Even so, I call out to this pack of clowns, 'Steady on, you clumsy yobs! Can't you see you'll drop Sister Bernadette, and if you do, your conscience and history will never let you forget,' to show I am standing in for Reverend Mother. But Benedict is superfluous by now. These toiling males are only doing one of the duties expected of the Force. They are rescuing an elderly bush walker who has given cause for concern by losing herself in the Blue Mountains.

As they mount the rise, globules of sweat bound off the

rescuers' skins and can almost be heard hissing as the earth swallows them up. A risen sun answers the ear-drums like a struck gong.

Benedict herself has become somewhat sweaty around the thyroid glands. She might have torn off her veil if it hadn't been for these uninitiated males acting so professional. And then, the other side of the ridge, Angela, Mary, Narelle appear, so 'nice' in their drip-dry summer tartans (two inches below the knee). They whimper with relief on sighting the cortège. The bearers are only too glad of a spell. They lay the stretcher on a narrow belt of level ground. The girls fall on their knees, regardless of damage to their lisle stockings. They kiss the hands of an ancient nun they have known distantly as Sister Bernadette. They chafe the milky skin to warm it in what is already a heatwave.

Benedict advises, 'Don't crowd her, girls. Let her have air. Air is what she needs.' What utter rot.

And now Benedict is more than ever superfluous, for here is Finbarr, of freckled, pollarded hands, and that pervading *red* smell ...

As the march is resumed; pork-skinned policemen, stumbling schoolgirls, and two attendant nuns, Finbarr is marching on the right hand, Benedict, she realises only too bitterly, on the left.

Finbarr has begun, in low key, and humble contralto tone, a prayer to the Mother of God.

What can the superfluous Benedict contribute beyond ineffectual tears? Her eyes are blinded by this most recent humiliation. She would have fallen if she hadn't grabbed a policeman by the biceps.

'Won't you try one of these sandwiches, Mother? They're

that bloater paste you love – from Fortnum's. I discovered some of it at D.J.'s. I must say it cost the earth,' my daughter informs us to draw attention to her thriftiness and at the same time her filial devotion.

'It would stick in my throat after that raw kipper, which admittedly was going off before we started out.'

We are into one of these picnics Hilda loves to organise, in the Park. She has invited Patrick, to make an audience for her attempt at glorification and witness of what she has to suffer.

'They look delicious,' says Patrick, falling in with her plan.

I must admit the sandwiches are exquisitely made. Patrick helps himself with a daintiness appropriate to Hilda's design.

'What do you mean by kipper?' Hilda inquires with the directness of a bulldozer bearing down on its victim.

'You wouldn't understand. I've been through quite an ordeal – in the course of things.'

Silence in the Park, broken at last by Patrick remarking between munches, 'Delicious. A dash of lemon, perhaps?'

Hilda smiles for his distinguished palate, and gratitude for recognition of her talent.

Oh, balls, balls, and lemon coughdrops!

Our food is spread on one of those tables installed by the Park authorities for the convenience of picnickers, and students who like to write their theses at them. The tables are bolted to concrete blocks to ensure permanence, but every so often, members of the public in a fit of *joie de vivre*, or, hate uproot a table and hurl it into the muddy waters of the lake.

I feel almost strong enough to uproot the table at which

we are sitting and hurl it into the lake beside us, inspired less by hatred than the despair and frustration of any woman, man, person up against the Hildas – and Patricks (yes, I've got to include Hilda's stooge) of the rational world.

'I don't understand what is wrong with you, Mother, on such an idyllic day.'

Old Patrick sits munching, eyelids lowered, refusing to be sucked into controversy.

Oh well, this is it. Let's face it. I can feel my strength of purpose melting into apathetic melancholy.

In the distance I catch sight of the Mystic and Dog going through the garbage which has spilled out of one of the pebbled concrete vases intended for rubbish, and which dogs, derelicts, and ibis can never leave alone.

I hear the sound of muffled choking in my congested throat.

My interest in these two beings in the middle distance attracts Hilda's attention.

'Yes, I admit it's a disgusting sight. But what can we do about it? We're not responsible for every human derelict and stray mongrel dog.'

'I'm responsible for my own garbage – my own rotten *soul*.'

At mention of the dirty word Hilda's face assumes its McDermott expression. She folds her upper lip over the lower. She bunches fingertips together to remove any crumbs from her flat front.

As she and Patrick carry on with the picnic they must consider I have done my best to ruin, I am seized by a brainwave. That is not the word, surely. My future has never appeared so determined, or more likely to appease my daughter.

'I haven't told you, Hilda, but I'll be going away before very long.'

'Oh, where?' she doesn't sound all that interested.

'I have an engagement with a theatre company. A really fantastic project – Arts Council funded – to take culture to the outback.'

'And what will you be expected to do?'

'Play some of Shakespeare's more interesting characters – both female and male. I'm going home to study them in a minute. You can't expect me to sit here all afternoon eating bloater sandwiches. And then, I've also been asked to contribute some of my Dolly Formosa monologues and dances.'

'Dolly Formosa?'

'Oh, yes. You wouldn't know about her, Hilda, because you've never taken any interest in my theatre perform-ances. You are one of those who dismiss theatre as illusion, when many of us see it as far more real than what is known as life. *Dolly Formosa and the Happy Few* is what I call my programme. Sounds élitist, doesn't it, Patrick? Lots will dis-miss it for that reason. You, Patrick, the most élite of élitists, should applaud if you would let yourself.'

I have almost run out of breath.

'As for the traditionalists, the "bardolators", there will be my Viola, Titania, Hamlet, Lear, my Rosalind, above all, my *Cleopatra*, in excerpts from the plays.'

Suddenly the Park is aglow with fevers of blue and green, the water is all glancing light and imperious swans.

'Well, I must leave you ... study – study – so many lines to cram into my head ... Dolly Formosa, of course, is second nature.'

They have finished their sandwiches. Hilda hands Patrick

a lettuce leaf, for his health, and what I can see will be a sour plum.

Study! Study! Study isn't the word for it.

I have Grandfather Gray's folio edition. The silver-fish have got into it. There are lines missing here and there. But many are superfluous, like so many of one's overheated thoughts.

Hilda looks in occasionally. 'Well, I don't believe any of it. But if it's true . . .'

'What is true except sincerity and great art?'

'I don't know how you dare, Mother. You've had no formal education.'

'Neither of us has. That's what rankles with you, Hilda. The difference is that I am an artist.'

She primps and purses. I hope she will soon leave me to the folio edition. There's so much to accomplish in a short time.

'I wish you success,' she says before going, in accents which let you know her hopes are for your disaster. 'What about the other members of this – company?'

'Various little *persons* – students and – mediocrities. So much will depend on me.'

'But men, Mother. How can you possibly get away with Hamlet?'

'Bernhardt did – and Esmé Bérenger.'

'As for Lear . . .'

'No male actor has ever conveyed the essence of Lear. He hasn't the necessary compassion. Lear will be all right. I'm insisting on a straw Cordelia. After that, you're home when the button's undone. You'll see . . . the house will be one big purge.'

'I can't bear to think about it.'

'You couldn't. You're too dry. You belong to Brenda McDermott country.'

'She isn't Brenda. She's Elspeth.'

'Ten times worse. Sounds like some woman radio announcer. How did you find out?'

'I saw it in her passport. She asked me if I thought the photograph was anything like.'

'And was it?'

'I hate to tell you ... Yes!'

Notes

p. 77   *tagari*: carry-all
          kouros: youth

p. 78   *skala*: port

p. 79   *horta*: herbs, weeds
          ambelourgikós: vine-grower

p. 81   Meera: Fate

p. 87   derro: Aust. sl. for derelict

p. 103   Burlington Bertie: popular music-hall song sung by Australian-born transvestite star, Ella Shields, in London and New York
          Fred: Astaire

p. 104   St Kilda: Melbourne suburb

p. 113   *trahaná*: soup made from dried ewes' milk
          galatoboúriko: pudding made from milk, semolina and honey
          nounoú: sl. wet-nurse

Editor's Remarks

As her preparations for the tour grew more intensive, Alex locked herself in her room. At first she refused food, but finally allowed Hilda to bring snacks to her door: salami, pickled cucumbers, *pastourmá*, yoghurt, and potato salad. The recluse would slam the door and re-lock it. When the time came round for the next meal, dirty dishes would be standing on the mat outside – a rare Bokhara saddle-bag somewhat smeared with mayonnaise.

Sometimes through a crack in the opened door Hilda would ask how the actress was progressing with her studies.

'Oh, fine, fine! They'll lap up my Cleopatra. Many great names have barged up the Nile but nobody has understood that Egyptian whore-slut. All those Anglo-Saxon ladies – pooh! In red wigs – or American accents. I *am* Cleopatra. I *know*. I have the smell of Egyptian women in my nostrils. I can hear their laughter – the clang of brass above running water. No *eau de Nil* – dirty water – bilharzia – the lot! You know what the key to Cleopatra is? She hung on to her clitoris. You should appreciate my Cleo, Hilda. She's real.'

It was never clear to anybody when the tour was expected to begin. There were references to rehearsals in a corrugated iron shed in the suburbs. As time went by and tension increased, Hilda asked, 'When will you be leaving us, Mother?'

'Soon, soon! The exact date hasn't been decided, the schedule is still being worked out.'

'Have you a contract?'

'Their word is their bond. It's the Arts Council.'

'I hope everything will be alright.'

'Oh, you needn't worry. One day you'll find I've gone. Gary will have fetched me – in the van.'

'Gary?'

'The director-manager. Could be Barry. Or even Craig. Wayne? There seem to be several Waynes around.'

'If I only knew the date, I'd pack a basket – a few little comforts for the road.'

'Comforts? Austerity is the keynote of our project.'

She shut the door as tight as she could.

Speaking from the other side, she continued, 'I'll keep Patrick posted on our progress. Patrick understands the demands of art, though he's never exactly come good himself. Patrick is too piss-elegant by half.'

From then on, the door remained shut between us. Had the genius removed herself? There were faint sounds. A scratching of mice. Once or twice a mewing as from one of the Empress Alexandra's cats. There were smells – of cheese, of Nescafé, and a spirit lamp.

I was away in Europe much of this time, but Hilda remitted letters from Ms Gray which amounted to a journal of the actress's progress through the outback.

Alex Gray's Theatrical Tour of Outback Australia

Dear Patrick,

We started off on the first stage of our journey into the wastes of Philistia. As it was early morning I was able to escape my daughter's advice. Through a cold and windy dawn my beloved cats wound down towards the gate piteously mewing after their defecting mother. I cried a little and at once realised I had forgotten tissues. Craig produced some. He is immensely considerate of his leading lady. Attractive thighs – but no use.

I drive with Craig in the first of our four vans. Craig is our director. He won't be any bother, because I made it clear at rehearsals that my performances, while formally structured, depend on my creative instinct for the drift of nuance and the fleshing out of character. You, Patrick, will understand immediately what Craig only finally accepted.

Craig and I are the only occupants of Van No. 1. Gary and Barry (sound, lighting, and general purposes) travel in No. 2, along with props, and all that angular, splintery stuff which will be put to many uses as it becomes transformed into settings of luxury and exotic beauty.

Other members of the company seem perfectly happy to squeeze into Nos 3 and 4. Most of these young people show great vitality and enthusiasm. They enjoy *closeness*, which is all to the good in the circumstances. One sulky little thing – Linda – may give trouble before very long.

She has ideas above her billing. But I have no doubt firmness and tact will deal with Linda if the need arises.

They have rigged up a bed for me at the back of our van where I can recline during the more tedious stretches of the journey, and my God how many of them there are, dust and trees, trees and dust, or simply dust. I lie amongst my sumptuous costumes, their velvets and brocades, the trappings of Athens, Egypt, and Illyria, attempting to protect them from the glare and mediocrity of the Australian bush. Sometimes I am carried off into dreams. I am standing in a robe of midnight velvet holding a great black fan of sequined net, I am about to launch into a role which has not yet been devised, although I can feel it forming in me. Incorporate it perhaps into Dolly Formosa's dance sequences and reveries.

When suddenly I am brought to my senses. I am tossed several feet in the air, my skull makes contact with the roof of the van. My God, I am concussed, if not fractured!

Craig calls back, 'No worries. We've just hit an interloping kangaroo.'

That's all very well. I could be maimed. Shall I sue the Council? Or will it be punishment enough if I am unable to perform at Cutncumagen? (I must remember little Linda, though – waiting to jump in and make the most of an emergency.)

Patrick darling,

Patience is the secret of life on the road, and magnanimity. I have become quite attached to some of my fellow actors, and they to me – I like to think. Even little Linda has her sulk-free moments. She shared a Mars Bar

with me yesterday while Barry, Gary and Craig were skin-
ning their knuckles changing a tyre on Van No. 2. Actually, if one is prepared to wait, some amiable brute of a
farmer will appear from beyond the horizon and do the
job in no time at all.

So far there is a drama attached to each town (*sic*) on
our schedule, but I shan't bore you with these stories unless
they are very special. Actually, there is a sameness about
the stories as there is about the towns. I can't go on writing
(*sic*) because there is almost too much *sic* about this journey.
(Oh dear, when I thought I had learnt humility while
playing an assortment of nuns, or just from living with an
impossibly dictatorial daughter. It seems I shall never be
humble. Are artists ever?)

There is a subtle difference about the sameness of the
towns (...) difficult to analyse – whether Peewee Plains,
Lone Coolabah, Ochtermochty, Kanga Kanga, Toogood,
Baggary Baggary, or Aberpissup – some nuance of civic
pride or absence of it, a clump of dusty cannas or bed of
burnt-out salvia, a row of dying or living poplars.

Dust is *everywhere*. I *know* every cranny of the School of
Arts by heart. The smell of every urinal or dunny. The
figure one may bump into in the dark.

When we started out I was told that members of the
company would be billeted with private families in each
town. I refused this warm offer, insisting that a room be
booked for me at the Royal, the Imperial, the Commercial,
or whatever. I love the iron-lace balconies. I love to limber
up by running a leg along the rail, regardless of the gratuitous audience in the street below, whereas in a private
home the hostess is worrying about her savoury boats, her
sponges and Pavlovas for the after-performance supper in

her lounge room. I know every lounge room from Cutn-cumagen to Ochtermochty. I know every balcony of every Imperial or Royal Hotel. At Ochtermochty – no, wait – I think it was Lone Coolabah – the balcony had been carried away by fire. I almost lost my balance, lifting my leg to limber up against the darkness. I could have toppled with disastrous results into my devoted audience in the street below.

Need I say that reactions to performances vary in any theatre, School of Arts, salon, or convent refectory through-out the world. You are a seasoned performer as I am.

The audience is puzzled by much of what I do, which I take as a tribute to creativity. Who wants to go on seeing the same old boring Rosalind, Viola, Hamlet, Lear, for ever? Mind you, most of the deprived individuals we play to haven't seen any of these characters in any shape or form. Not like the professional 'bardolators' in the capital cities of this colony.

Sometimes creatures, always at the back of the hall, shout rudery such as, 'If the guy's supposed to be fat and short of breath 'e shouldn't look skinny as an old ewe on agistment,' or, 'Why's the lady carryin' the straw dolly got whiskers tied on under 'er chin?' In such cases the mayor, or at least an alderman, has to go round and silence them, or if that doesn't work, ask them to leave. Sometimes that doesn't work either. At Peewee Plains there were eggs and tomatoes: quite a scandal.

Patrick,

You will wonder why there's been a pause in my report on our progress. It is not that I'm deterred by rebuffs. Isn't it what we expect when we lay our necks on the block for art? If the axe falls, the blood may reach *somebody* and dragons' teeth spring up to defend our cause.

Anyway ...

What may prove to be the historic climax of our tour came at Ochtermochty. Or was it Baggary Baggary? Frankly I'm too dazed to remember. The *Sydney Morning Herald* had promised to fly their critic, K.V.H., to cover our performance. They kept their promise! K.V.H. landed at dusk in a Cessna. He was driven to the Royal, Imperial, or Commercial for a wash and brush-up, the usual armpit drill, before the Mayor turned up to drive him to the hall. No time for more than a ham sandwich, but it was hoped he would be elegantly fed at the post-performance supper.

At the Royal, Imperial or Commercial I could hear the Critic freshening himself at the washstand. He was embarrassingly close to the star. I was too discreet to knock at his door and tip him off to my potentialities, as no doubt many would have done – nibbled at the opposite end of his ham sandwich till they met in the middle, brushed away the dandruff from his coat collar.

Enfin, I am not as others ...

Discussing the event with members of the company before what turned out a disastrous evening, none of us could think what the initial in the centre of the cluster stood for. We were all familiar with King Harry, but that V ... Linda, who is a bitch, but a nice one when she is on side, suggested the V could stand for Vampire, except that K.V.H. might have shown more signs of the blood he has sucked.

We enjoyed a giggle as we slapped on the make-up. In my case, as Cleopatra, a lengthy operation – to suggest the earthiness, the Nile silt, the *ful medames* of which this

Egyptian slut is composed. I reflected how my mother-in-law Magda Demirjian, herself a Middle Eastern slut, would have appreciated the transformation. I could not help feeling pleased with myself as my glance roamed from dirty navel to bloody talons and ditto toenails – except the one whose toe had got jammed in a door. I was ready for King Vampire Harry of the *Sydney Morning Herald* – to challenge 'bardolatry' with truth.

The programme started with scenes from some of the comedies performed by supporting actors. Poor things, I could hear the yawns from where I sat brooding over the missing toenail, waiting to project my interpretation of Cleopatra at an audience which might, or might not, be won over – including K.V.H. of the *S.M.H.* To pass the time I composed snatches of the notices I might receive: '... unorthodox to say the least. But do we expect orthodoxy from a great creative artist? No Bernhardt, no Duse, Ms Gray stands on her own – she flows rather, as rhythmically as the waters of the Nile. If the audience was puzzled at times by what she offered, they may understand in retrospect the experience through which they lived that night in Ochtermochty. For me it will remain a landmark in the theatre of the unexpected ...'

I was in a slight sweat by the time I made my appearance. Considering the poetic realism of my interpretation sweat only enhanced my portrayal of the Egyptian Queen. After the first shock when I made my entrance, excerpt followed excerpt smoothly enough with all these sweet, enthusiastic young people doubling and quadrupling in my support. In the circumstances, sound and lighting effects were a bit off-key, and some of the yobbos at the back of the hall enjoyed the humour more than the poetry. Once or twice I caught sight of the Critic's face (so unmistakably pallid) surrounded by the official party.

Craig had introduced the play, obviating all those (to my mind) tedious battles with which Shakespeare litters his work, and explained that we were concentrating on the tremendous scene of Cleopatra's death which is in fact the *raison d'être* of this epic drama. (I had coached him carefully and I must say dear old Craig made his point very elegantly.)

With much clatter of hardware and actors swirling on and off, we conveyed the hurlyburly of war in a series of economical but credible impressions. Men, men and more men (sometimes women in disguise). Considering the burden our actresses had to bear in an almost wholly masculine cast, I persuaded the director to cut the role of Octavia, an insipid character any way you look at her. No one could accuse *me* of having it in for Octavia, when Cleopatra herself shared my opinion. Octavia is dispensable.

For that matter I could have dispensed with some of the men – Caesar with those thin shanks covered with a fuzz of sandy fur, and alas, a *puny* Antony, graduated from NIDA a couple of months before the tour.

My aura, even when Cleopatra is off stage, had to authenticate some of Shakespeare's more sensuous visions – indifferently painted here by mediocre artists:

> *The barge she sat in, like a burnished throne,*
> *Burned on the water: the poop was beaten gold,*
> *Purple the sails, and so perfumèd that*
> *The winds were lovesick with them . . .*

VOICE FROM THE DARK: . . . a great play sacrificed to vanity . . .

Or:

> *Age cannot wither her, nor custom stale*
> *Her infinite variety; other women cloy*
> *The appetites they feed . . .*

Nobody could ever deny that – no husband, lover – not even my daughter Hilda Gray.

VOICE FROM THE DARK: Talk, talk, talk . . . Oh, Gawd! This is where I nip out and knock back a few at the old Imperial . . .

I confess there are *longueurs*. I drift for stretches on a river of words and memories. I shall never forget the look of terror in Antony's eyes as my tongue planted a kiss between his parted lips. Poor boy, the Lindfield in him could not take it. The slimy Nile aspic might have entered before its cue. Men and words . . . I float on the waters of frustrated passion and poetry between the mud banks which contain my life. So, roll on the aspic! I do not dread the asp for the end it brings, but for the performance.

My stalwart women, Charmian/Linda and Iras/Sue Mk II, will not let me down. Not even in hauling Antony up into the Monument, their sinewy arms nearly dropped, then recovered him.

It is the Clown Countryman I dread. This WAYNE. I could have done it so much better, and cannot prevent myself letting him see it. Wayne was unendurable from the moment I set eyes on him emerging in a not-so-muscular T-shirt from Van No. 4. Let it be said however, no Wayne is to be endured. O Wayne, O wine, full of sediment and dubious cork . . .

The moment is here!

RE-ENTER GUARD, WITH A CLOWN (BRINGING IN A BASKET).
GUARD: *This is the man (sic). He brings your figs.*
CLEOPATRA: *Avoid and leave him.*
               Hast the pretty worm of Nilus there,
               That kills and pains not?

Don't get it into your head, Wayne, that you'll spare me pain, I all but mutter.

CLOWN/COUNTRYMAN: *Truly I have him . . .*
                         . . . his biting is immortal: those who die of it do seldom or never recover.

Understand if you can, Wayne, the irony in what you speak

so on so on so on doh doh de doh

CLEOPATRA: *Get thee hence, farewell.*
CLOWN: *I wish you all joy of the worm.* (SETS DOWN HIS BASKET.)
CLEOPATRA: *Farewell.*
CLEOPATRA: (between her teeth) *Urghhh, get thee gone, get thee gone – Wayne.*

Now at last my reliable girls are with me alone. I have almost forgotten the audience.

CLEOPATRA: (applying asp to her breast) *Come thou mortal wretch ...*

VOICE FROM THE DARK: She won't get bit. There's nothing to bite on.

Though some sniggered, I could tell the majority of the audience resented this insult to one who has always been considered voluptuous (envied even by her Demirjian mother-in-law). I am not deterred.

CLEOPATRA: *Peace, peace!*
Dost thou not see my baby at my breast,
That sucks the nurse asleep!

VOICE: Rock-a-bye – boo-hoo-hoo!

CLEOPATRA: *As sweet as balm, as soft as air, as gentle.*
O, Antony! Nay I will take thee too
    (applies another asp to her arm).
What should I stay ...   (DIES).

I lie half-dead in life. Forget the rest – Caesar with sandy, fuzzy shanks – of the McDermott clan perhaps? All all is pointless.

We took our calls to sparse, but frantic applause and I looked forward to meeting K.V.H. at the post-performance supper in the Mayor's own lounge room, where I was confident of dispelling any reservations he might have had about the performance. Imagine my disappointment when, after ridding myself of the Nile silt, and arriving still reeking of coconut butter, I was told the Critic had been forced to return to his paper, to write his review. The Cessna had taken off.

Reviews ... we both know about them, Patrick, do we

not? You will have read K.V.H. on Cleopatra. Because our friends always point out the bad ones while overlooking the good.

That K.V.H. found my Cleopatra 'very, very funny' did not hurt me as much as my enemies would hope. What did distress me – momentarily – was his remark that he did not stay for Ms Gray's monologues *Dolly Formosa and the Happy Few* because he might have found them 'too, too modern'. Understandable of course when you and I know that the Critic's last gesture to modernity was many years ago when he invented Brecht.

I performed *Dolly Formosa* the second night at Ochtermochty. I was determined not to chicken out and move on immediately to Aberpissup as the management and some of the company favoured. I would give my all in this blighted little corner of Philistia. The Mayor was rather sweet (he pinched my bottom during supper) and his wife had slaved so nobly at the buffet the Critic walked out on.

Linda and I took refuge at first in the bathroom. A haven of pastel blue and pink. Linda, somewhat smashed, fell into the bath. An emissary arrived, jiggling the doorknob for me to come and cut the Pavlova prepared in my honour. I managed to extricate Linda from the bath and our hostess's shower cap, not before she had torn off a tap. We were more or less presentable on arriving at the buffet. In any case most of the guests were well away on the punch the Mayor was ladling out. As for the Pavlova, it was a masterpiece of the Country Woman's craft. A passion-fruit seed made straight for the only hollow tooth in my head and stayed there to martyrise me.

I made a little speech. I – *we* – loved everybody in Ochtermochty for taking us so readily to their hearts etc. etc.

I lay awake half the night crying my heart out on an already damp pillow, under the honeycomb bedspread at the Royal-Imperial-Commercial, while somebody at intervals tried the door-knob.

Most of the following day I lay on my bed. At least the door-knob had calmed down. I rose towards evening and took stock of myself in the deal dressing-table glass. I looked interestingly ravaged, ageless, ready to do battle with art and life.

Grave misgivings at the School of Arts. Craig remains loyal. He kisses me and chafes my body from the rear, to give me the courage I only momentarily need. Barry and Gary are there for sound and lighting, but the auditorium is ominously dark. I see figures distributed here and there through the stalls, like soft sculpture in crêpe shrouds – presumably members of the company, with the exception of Linda, who has stayed smashed, I am told, ever since she played Charmian to my Cleopatra. From the back row I can already hear the braying of the jackass, waiting to worry my words every time an opportunity offers.

Do they think I am simple enough to give them these opportunities? If they could not understand the language of Shakespeare, why waste on them the complexities of Dolly Formosa's thoughts? I decide to confine my performance to dance, to those movements which have already begun to inspire my limbs.

When I stride out centre stage I am wearing my midnight robe. I am carrying the great black fan of sequined net. I introduce myself quite simply to the soft sculpture forms of my audience: 'Dolly Formosa welcomes you to-night, her Happy Few in appreciating art and life.'

By now I scarcely know whether the lighting and the tape which accompany my performance are controlled by technicians. The iron roof has slid back and my sequined fan and midnight robe are in correspondence with the galaxy.

I move magnificently in time with the rhythm of the earth. No matter that several of the sticks of my fan have broken, or that the net is reduced to dusty tatters under stress from the emotions which possess me.

One of the jackasses at the back seizes the opportunity to bray, 'Good on yer, missus! Never seen the like in all my days . . .' I should think he hasn't.

But the Happy Few will understand, as I shed my mid-night robe, and my naked body conjures up the archetypes of birds, serpents, insects, many of them fiendish in their savage beauty, all hatched out of Dolly Formosa's teeming brain. I sink down exhausted at last into the earth from which we have come and to which we shall return.

Craig? Gary? Barry? one of them supports me so that I can take my call.

I hear a cry ' . . . it's a shame – the Government ought to protect decent people from such indecent rot!' and from another quarter, 'Why don't they send us something like *How to Succeed in Business*?'

I need no support. I have my convictions my belief in truth. If I hobble it's because I must have trodden on a tack. It is not surprising that I have gooseflesh. The evil blast of popular ill-will is trained on my nakedness, and the draught from an open door hits me in the pubics.

*   *   *

However long or short, chilly or stifling, the rest of the night, I rose before dawn. I put on one of those grey shifts which I have always found adapt themselves to any situation. I walk barefoot, down the creaking stairs, along the sticky hotel lino, stained by grease, alcohol, semen, and wine, past the stagnating kitchen where the cockroaches are at play in the pans of leftover cabbage and mash, congealing snags, and chuck steaks waiting to be transformed into a tasty lunchtime braise.

Loathsome as it all was the somnolent hotel seemed to accept me as an extension of itself, a detail in its reflections of human nature and the putrescence which living breeds.

O God! I don't know why I should invoke the name of one who probably does not exist.

As I stepped out across the rotting floor-boards of the hotel veranda, through the cracks in which sink-water is already steaming, the sun has started rising across the plain. My feet are excoriated by the stones on the surface of what passes for a street.

I walk on into the plain beyond, a carpet of dust, almost a mattress. A few ghost trees console the revenant I have become. Small birds skitter across the desert, larger ones rise by grace of a stately basketwork of wings. I bow my head under the increasing weight of heat, my eyes humbled by the sheets of metallic light opening out, swingeing at me from the distance. If I were at least a shadow, but I am not, I am nothing now that my ghost trees have evaporated in heat and glare. Not even an insect. Louse fallen from a bird's wing. Grain of mica.

I drop to my knees. My tears are molten as they pour from sockets sunk deep into my leathery cheeks.

Then I look up and he is kneeling opposite in exactly

the same position. We are a few yards apart. I cannot see his face, because it is gilded by the sun's glare, but sense that it is smiling, and know that it must be as dark as the smooth dark kneeling thighs. I can feel the stream of understanding which flows from this miraculous Being, bathing my shattered body, revitalising my devastated mind.

The vans are drawn up outside the hotel. Props and costumes must already have been collected from the School of Arts by the back-stage team. The less responsible members of the company are drifting out of side streets from their billets, laden with belongings: garments which mutate depending on climate and circumstances, photographs, mascot-toys, make-up, a tarot pack, cigarettes, dope, and parcels of sandwiches put up by hostesses grateful for the favour they believe culture has done them.

Some of the actors' possessions are dropped and retrieved, dropped and retrieved, from the gritty street. The heat encourages indolence. I see amongst those taking part in the movements of this languid dance, Barry, Gary, Craig, Sue Mk I, Mk II, a Robin or two – WAYNE. The only John in the company, my Antony, as straight as Lindfield makes them, has always tried to look through me as though I did not exist, so it is no surprise that he should do so now.

Linda shows up, blowing gum-bubbles, trailing a kimono by one sleeve. Linda, too, does not seem to know me, when we have enjoyed moments of intimacy at various stations of our journey. Her eyes look unusually pale; perhaps the glare prevents her recognising the person approaching. She climbs up beside Craig, in the passenger seat of Van No. 1. His thin, rather hairy arms set the van in motion.

I wonder who will inherit my midnight robe and sequined fan. Or have I never existed for any of them? They drive on to Aberpissup, is it? Toogood? Baggary Baggary? No matter which, for their offerings from the safer Shakespeare.

I stoop and pick up a snapshot lying in the middle of the street. The figure at least is mine, limbs daubed with Nile silt, crimson talons, lacquered toenails, except for the one removed by jamming in a door. But the face has come out blurred, it could be anybody's.

Notes

p. 129   *ful medames*: Egyptian beans
p. 132   Lindfield: very respectable suburb on Sydney's north side
p. 138   snags: Aust. sl. for sausages

Editor's Remarks

Hilda and I were sitting in the deck-chairs on the tiled veranda overlooking the Park. She has fixed my chair as close as possible to an upright position, knowing that arthritis makes it difficult for me by now to get to my feet even with help from a stick. Hilda is as considerate of infirmity as her mother deplores any such consideration, refusing to accept sickness and age.

I asked Hilda how Alex passes the time.

She laughed. 'You've had her account of the famous tour. Even if it took place only in her mind, I hope she will have learnt a lesson. It should have got theatre out of her system.'

From the performer in myself I was not so sure. Hilda is, in so many respects, an innocent.

'Anyway, life here has been peaceful. I've fed her whenever she showed she wanted it. I listen for sounds. The cats keep me pretty well informed about what's going on upstairs. They don't like me any more than she does, but they're a useful source of leakage.'

Poor Hilda, who always wanted so much to be liked.

At this point one of the cats, was it old Trifle?, or the more recent, youthful Tyger, pushed between the sliding, screen doors separating living room from veranda. Tyger flashed the stranger a yellow glare. He gave a soundless mew, withdrew his tongue, and shambled on. His woolly

pants were shameless in their arrogance, his anus an immaculate rosette.

I was not altogether surprised when, soon after, the
screen doors opened slightly wider and Alex herself
squeezed through without an effort. Hilda swears her
mother is suffering from anorexia. To me she simply pulls
herself together at intervals, and enjoys the sensual pleasure
of running her hands down her sides, over rib-cage, hips,
thighs, of a figure perfect for its age.

Her naked lips offered us a thin smile, as disbelieving as
the one we should have returned. Fond as I am of Alex, I am
so bad at portraying the social emotions – like Alex herself.

She began by saying, 'You know all about the tour,
Patrick, because Hilda is too honest not to have forwarded
my account of it.'

'Yes, I know something of it.' I had to admit.

'And will believe, or disbelieve, as much of the truth we
both have learnt to accept.'

'Of course,' I answer.

At the same time I try to propel myself out of the chair
with the help of my stick in deference to one I so much
admire.

'Don't, Patrick,' she advised.

She draws out a little do-it-yourself stool-table with
scruffy mat which has beeen standing centre against the
veranda wall for the convenience of her cats when they
indulge in bird- or stranger-watching from the sphinx position.

She seated herself on the edge of this cheap furniture.
She was wearing a simple ageless suit in bleached linen
which matched her mood perfectly.

'Surely not Chanel?'

'Who else? She lasts for ever if you're not foolish enough to give her to St Vincent de Paul or the Opportunity Shop.'

She is without jewels. She notices me looking her over and my glance focused at last on the wedding ring.

'Something one can't get rid of. I've been the bride so often I'm keeping it for the final mistake.'

Silence falls. One wonders how she has ended up amongst the asters, the petunias, the phlox, the silver-eyes and bulbuls of suburbia.

I try to turn our attention from the reality of our immediate surroundings to the fantasy life we have helped her create for herself.

'At least you've got through your theatrical tour without any obvious wounds.'

'If they're not obvious, that's all to the good. I wouldn't hide them from you or anybody else. I have always respected what is real.'

Again a silence, broken only by birds and plants.

'It was an experience, to say the least. I met some entrancing kids,' her teeth masticating the term were those of a true gourmet of language. 'They understood me – I think – as many of you don't.'

She looked at us and away with the pursed mouth and pouting cheeks of a child expecting the grown-ups to accuse her of what they call an un-truth.

She might have been preparing to blow a raspberry in our faces, but I didn't give her time.

'Now that you're rested, I expect you're preparing for a next – a different phase in your never-ending career.'

Rested she certainly looked. She might have spent the whole of her 'tour' sitting upstairs, buffing her nails,

brushing and touching up her immaculate helmet of youthful hair, then getting into the Chanel suit for her entrance
on the veranda to impress her captive audience of two.

I might have caught her out. Hilda looked as though she
thought I was being dishonest.

Alex only hesitated a second, sighed, and squared her
Chanel shoulders. 'Actually, the theatre hasn't washed me
up. I've been engaged by the Sand Pit. I have a contract
for small parts and walk-ons.'

She sat rocking on the edge of the do-it-yourself table,
tapping the toe of a court shoe against the veranda tiles.
The glacé shoe's rat-a-tat on terracotta specked with grey-
white sparrow droppings, insisted on the truth of what she
had told us.

She laughed, exposed her throat to Heaven and blurted,
'They say bird shit brings luck!'

Overhead, tunnels of spiders' web, grey and dusty as
geriatric armpits and pubics.

I didn't know about the Sand Pit, I had to confess.

'Strange, when it's never out of the news. Innovative
theatre – so-called. The audience is confounded by actors
rising up live out of the sand where they must have been
buried for what seems like several hours.'

'Nothing innovative in sand. Beckett used it years ago.'

'And will go on till he's ground humanity down to its
last grain of significance. The Chinese Emperors dropped
to the possibilities of sand long before Beckett. They buried
their entourage live in the stuff. Then, what about the
Desert Fathers? They recognised the mortifying properties
of sand. And with due respect to all of them Alex Gray
accepts sand, silence, and nothingness as the possible way
to something more positive than life.'

She paused, perhaps to enjoy my surprise. She was never much of a scholar, while always ready to exalt her instinct.

Through a grille of teeth, yellower than we had noticed earlier, she added a few last words to her lecture, 'I know from having spent much of my life up to the neck in burning sand – by choice, I should say – when not buried completely and forcibly by my Chinese torturers. Now you will tell the world I am mad!'

On this note of triumph she left us to what she saw as our distress.

I am now so busy at the Sand Pit the events I record can only appear erratic impressions. Perhaps I misread my contract, but I did not realise some of my roles at the theatre would be those of barmaid and lavatory cleaner. I don't know which is more difficult, dealing with actual excrement, or facing human shit the other side of the counter.

Shan't let on to Patrick and Hilda about these aspects of my life as an actor. Of course they may riffle through my papers behind my back, break into my writing-case however successfully I persuade myself I have hidden it. I believe neither of them knows about the priest hole under the eaves with its never-fading reek of dead possum and the Mystic's B.O. Age and arthritis have deprived Patrick of any but the wheelchair approach to exploration, but little Hilda has a nose for smells.

As my blue flesh mops and slops around through the stench of carbolic and urine, the hissing and pissing of the Sand Pit's stainless-steel lavatories, there's always the graffiti to enjoy: *If I'm up the director Monday no one can call me a poof cos I fuck me Auntie Friday night.* I have strict orders from the management to scrub it off, but it won't some-how come. Other info is more general: *You can't say herpes isn't a means of communication.* And no one can deny that charitable hearts aren't still around in this all-for-me society of ours: *Togetherness is a full bed ring Lady Mary Zipfinger 32432 at her million dollar Darling Point penthouse if you're looking for a good time* ... Mind you, I don't go along with porn, but you've got to agree that a larf is therapeutic.

Once when I had scarcely stripped off my pink rubber gloves, grabbed a wedge of quiche, and stationed my fall-ing arches behind the foyer bar, I caught sight of a ghost from the past.

'Isn't that you, Craig?' I called, recognising the sinewy, rather hairy arms and Byzantine beard of the manager-director of my Arts Council sponsored tour of the outback.

He looked at me as though he had never seen me before.

Well, one does meet an awful lot of people. Memory deludes as one grows older. But Craig isn't old. He ought to recognise.

He flicks his head. 'Gotter sort out the membership forms from the new set of free programmes.' He appeared harassed.

'Thought you'd be working backstage, Craig.'

It was only later, when he was chatting up some of the prettier foyer dollies and helping geriatric deformities mount the stairs that I realised he was an usher.

Or was it Craig? Any more than I am I?

Here is my little friend Linda. She at least will recognise me. Or will she? Perhaps she saw how hurt I was when she took over my seat next to the driver in Van No. 1 as they left Ochtermochty. Perhaps she and Craig fell out soon after. Tonight they seem bent on avoiding each other.

Sometimes I think it's a case of glass eyes. From observing people I believe almost everybody has one. Including myself. But nobody could have two, could they? I have heard my own eye go clunk as I drop it into Grandfather Gray's little agate cup which I have stood in the icon corner and where so many visitors (particularly friends) stub their cigarettes. I didn't know how anybody could mistake this little cup in transparent agate for an ashtray, standing as it is in front of the icons. Perhaps they wish to express their contempt for saints. Nobody could guess that this is where I drop my eye to give the socket a rest. They could, I suppose, have it in mind, and foresee how ash will irritate the socket when I replace my eyeball. Friends often know better than enemies how to hurt. This is why Hilda and I, who are worse than friends – mother and daughter – have such a disastrous effect on each other.

All this about glass eyes got into my head tonight on catching sight of my former friend Linda. I would not have expected her to recognise me straight off. Hair makes a lot of difference and tonight I have this gel stiffening my orange Mohican hair-do.

Going as Alice in Wonderland, poor Linda looks out of it beside the gelled-up barmaid. She is holding her escort by the biceps as he leads her towards the bar. Admittedly he's a real dish, but she needn't be holding him that tight, he shows no signs of wanting to escape. He is about to buy her a drink and a wedge of quiche or slice of our nutritious carrot cake. It is then I get the idea that Linda has, not one glass eye, but two. She could not have looked so glassy even if doped to the gills, as I knew from old she frequently is. I was longing to bring up Ochtermochty, Cutncumagen, Pee Wee Plains, Baggary Baggary et al. when the tall guy who is leading her turns to her and asks.

'What do you fancy, Edwina?'

And she answers without any hesitation, 'I could knock back a Margarita if I've got to sit through this lousy show.'

'Two Margaritas,' the guy orders, he has these dark side-burns, greying at the cheekbones.

'Won't you join us?' he asks the barmaid.

There was nothing I would have liked better, to down a couple of Margaritas, and end up swinging from the iron-grey bugger-grips, but I wasn't sure it was part of the management's policy for the barmaid to socialise with the customers so early in the evening.

So I gave him my nicest smile, and refused. After I'd fixed the Margaritas, running the salt round the rim of the glass as I had seen it done and pouring more tequila than I ought, I poured myself a glass of chlorinated tap water to show I meant to be sociable.

'An Indian friend', I confided, 'taught me years ago how to extract the *prana* from a glass of water.'

They both stared. I wondered whether I should have thrown in the 'years ago': they could have started seeing me as some old bag who had been on the India circuit, when this evening I was feeling so young and supple.

'And how do you', asks Linda/Edwina, 'extract whatever from a glass of water?'

'It's a matter of will power,' I reply.

Perhaps I sounded a bit smug. Anyway, they freeze as though I suspect them of something unmentionable.

I decided it was time to ask Linda about the tour.

'When I first set eyes on you,' I said, and may have dropped a clanger mentioning eyes, 'I was sure you were Linda – Smallwood, isn't it? The actress.'

'No, I'm Edwina.' She looked glassier than ever. 'Edwina's the name my mother gave me. I can't say I'm not an actress, though – on and off – more off than on,' she glares at me, 'like most of us.'

So I was put in my place.

Darcy, the friend (he's a real Darcy) makes some attempt at conversation.

But there's more in the air, I begin to sense, than the rigor mortis which has set in between a couple of actresses. For some time Cloris (she's the S.M.) has been stamping out through the foyer to the front entrance, and looking anxiously up and down the street. Something tells me an important actor hasn't turned up.

Chris – no, Clark (the director) appears and calls me out from behind the bar. What's this, I wonder? Is it because I haven't scrubbed the graffiti off their bloody old lavatory walls?

But no! 'Anne Brinkman-Smijth', he whispers, 'hasn't showed up, and it looks like she won't. We've called her at her Vaucluse home, and her parents' place at Jamberoo.'

'What of it?' I ask, trembling at every extremity.

'You can't say it's an important part. But a lot depends on it, Alex.'

I knew all about Anne Brinkman-Smijth (the j in Smith far more important than the part). She had a body, and could emote like nobody else in the business when she was in the mood.

'You, Alex, will have to stand in.'

'But I don't know the lines.'

'There's only one and it's unforgettable.'

Actually, I'd heard it, sailing out over and over at rehearsals.

'All you've got to say,' says Clark, 'is, "I am the spirit of the land, past, present, and future."'

He, and by now, Cloris, were dragging me towards the dressing room. They stripped me of my clothes and got me into the white mosquito-net nightie, a bit grey from sandpit sand, which Brinkman–Smijth wears for her part. They dragged me out into the still-deserted sandpit and began digging a grave. Normally I haven't a nerve in my body. I've been through so much.

'Now,' they explain, 'all you have to do is lie still, hold the snorkel in your mouth after you've been covered up, and listen for your cue. This will come from Brian . . .'

Brian is a big bushy Irish convict with marks of the cat all over his back.

'You'll hear his chains clink closer and closer, till he hollers, "So much for the humanity of English gentlemen and bullies." Then you spring up from out of the sand, deliver your line, and Benno here will whirl you round his shoulders.'

I was so confused, I let them push me into the grave and bury me alive, while I hung on for dear life to my cardboard exhaust pipe.

During the centuries which followed, there was much coming and going, and clanking of so many chains, I wondered whether I had missed my cue. I passed the time praying to Our Lady and the Panayia, not forgetting the Holy Ghost, and adding a few saints I remember from the Acts. I'm all for acts.

All of you, I pray from the depths of the grave, *I don't want to – DIE!*

My teeth must almost have bitten through the lower end of the snorkel, which added to my terror of death by asphyxiation. My itching eyeballs long to watch another sunrise through the holmoaks, palms, and bunya bunya pines, above the convents and the lone Protestant church, which screen the ocean. I *must* take part in another of those damp, salt-heavy dawns where the sticky hibiscus trumpets a hope which may or may not be fulfilled.

Mortal life, I am convinced, is more than I can sacrifice to an artistic death at the Sand Pit Theatre. If I don't get a move on, Benno's big black spongy heel may stamp out my limited air supply. So, regardless of whether I'm forestalling my cue I spring out shrieking, instead of the line I had been given, 'I am the Resurrection and the Life,' whereupon Benno, the archetype Aborigine from somewhere Wilcannia way, with a dash of Sephardic from the Gold Coast, grabs me and whirls me around his shoulders. The Sand Pit audience, each member probably an unbeliever on principle, is so startled by the unorthodox message, as well as my unexpected appearance, lets out a sustained gasp. Are they supposed to laugh? I suspect no one has ever dared at a venue for serious, innovative drama like the Sand Pit. But finally they can't contain themselves, and as Benno whirls me always higher towards the girders in my grotty mosquito-net, all-revealing nightie, the audience unites in the kind of roar which lays them in the aisles, theatre parties – and our less responsible critics – at Her Majesty's and the Royal.

God knows how it might have ended if . . .

As it happened, it ended on my own wrinkled bed, at what hour of morning I could not have told, except that outside the misted panes there was a corn-coloured moon in a sky of jacaranda blue. Corny. I don't doubt, but as real as anything that passes for reality. So I lay sobbing awhile amongst the estuaries and craters that many nights of self-doubt and despair had mapped on the sheet.

Then I got up. I had to read today's bulletin on myself before my daughter came in, gave me the once over, and let me know what I stood for in her eyes and those of the 'normal' world.

According to the vision of myself in the glass I could not be dismissed as a geriatric nut. Certainly ravaged, I still radiated the strength of will of those who are being saved up for some final scene in the terrifying theatre of life. You couldn't refer to 'death', as Hilda and Patrick might if they dared abandon their bourgeois discretion.

I raised my arms. They are still wiry enough to swing from a trapeze. Nests of little black snakes raise their heads from each armpit. I exercise my hands, my fingers. They are not so arthritic they could not handle a gun, take aim, and pull the trigger on a chosen target.

I can hear Hilda across the landing, turning in the last of her early morning dreams. I must hurry. I grab some liner from out of the chaos on my dressing-table top. I elongate the shape of my eyes. Why, I wonder? To give myself the confidence no one but myself knows I lack? Now I am the great archetypal bird who can face any darkness I'm expected to.

I try not to thump the stairs as I make my way down to the kitchen. Though without appetite, I must try to make a show of eating breakfast before Hilda arrives and forces something nauseating on me. I am too old to cope with morning sickness. She shouldn't object to my appearance. I am wearing a simple voile nightdress of long ago – nothing see-through about it. I help myself to a handful of cornflakes from the pantry, souse them in virtuous milk, and to give myself heart, add some of the cheap brandy Hilda keeps as a medicine, when, oh God, I smash the bottle by knocking it off the table. I dispose of the fragments of glass by shuffling them out of sight with my feet.

Hilda is coming. I hear her on the stairs. Nothing can be done in time about the spilt brandy, a dark amber lake laced with blood from my wounded feet spreading across the kitchen floor. I sit down hoping Hilda will not yet have rubbed the sleep from her eyes. I crouch above my doctored conflakes and milk.

'You've come down unusually early, Mother.'

'Well, I was awake, and it seemed the natural move on such a lovely day ...'

I am a little secretive girl to my daughter in her role as stern mother preparing to accuse her child of some unspecified behaviour which could only prove undesirable. I can feel the mingy little pigtails dangling trembling alongside my apprehensive cheeks.

Hilda strides around in her judicial robe. She too, probably, has to salvage confidence from out of the blurred world of sleep.

She begins suddenly, 'What's all this - liquid - on the floor?'

I stare stupidly round-mouthed down.

'It must be one of the cats -' I prevent myself coming out with 'Mummy', I manage to turn it into - 'darling.'

I can't believe she is convinced. She isn't. The whole kitchen is reeking of brandy.

But I persist, in desperation. 'I was so tired when I got home from the theatre, I just fell on my bed. And the poor incarcerated pets must have pissed on the floor. It's as simple as that.'

Hilda makes herself a cup of coffee – not real – Nescafé. She stirs it furiously with her spoon to show what she thinks of her little girl-mother, and possibly the world at large.

We sit at opposite sides of the table, pretending we are not paddling in brandy and broken glass.

'Surely by now you must have got rid of your theatre obsession?' she begins.

I gulp down a mouthful of brandied cornflakes. The brandy makes me feel more like myself.

'Actually, the Sand Pit has offered me parts in their next production. Not as important as those who admire my work feel that I deserve ... But who knows? A foot in the door is better than a jammed toe. It may lead to anything.'

I look at the watch I realise I am not wearing.

'We start rehearsing tomorrow. Or is it today? I must check with my engagement book.'

Hilda gets up grudgingly, to face dealing with glass splinters, brandy and blood.

I try to distract her attention from any such unpleasantness.

'I expect you'll be going out, won't you? To buy the lettuces – and rolled oats,' knowing she is still under the influence of Mrs Elspeth/Brenda McDermott.

She mumps a reply.

I help her in her work by standing the plate with its remains of soggy cornflakes beside the sink.

When I hear her ask, 'What is the theme of your play?'

I'm surprised that she should show such interest.

'Well ... Difficult to put it in a nutshell – like life itself. I'd say it unites all the great themes – classic and contemporary dilemmas. War. Corruption. Violence. Revolution.

Anarchy. Love and sex, in their many variations. The BOMB! Ashes . . .'

I can feel them on my lips along with the detritus of cornflakes – bitter, bitter . . .

Hilda appears unmoved.

However, she condescends to utter, 'What is its title?'

'*Nothing or Something*. On the other hand, it could be *Something or Nothing*. It will have to be worked out – by all of us – democratically – because we're a democratic group.'

'Oh.'

I slip away upstairs. The question is – should rehearsals begin today? Or tomorrow? There is no sign of a date in my little onion-skin diary. If tomorrow, it will give Hilda a chance to alert Patrick and perhaps call in Falkenberg if they decide things have gone far enough. So I decide to make the break this morning.

I wait till I hear her leave by the back gate on the lettuce and porridge run. I check my make-up box, and go through my shoulder bag to make sure that all my necessities are there (fewer and fewer of them as time goes on; I'm almost prepared to walk down the street naked, with a box of tissues under one arm, and a revolver snuggling into an armpit).

At the last moment I can't resist a gesture. I open the wardrobe and shake my dear old chinchilla from out of the moth-bag. Rather a gamble – it could condemn me to the pits with the company or, depending on luck and climate, elevate me to leading roles.

I call a taxi. Though the day will be a steamy one, I decide to wear the chinchilla. Safer than carrying it. And it will provide armour of a kind if the taxi-driver is a nark.

The cab slides alongside the fence. The man is neither young nor old, firmly fleshed of thigh and arm, wearing dark glasses, a cynical expression and Digger's hat.

'I adore the hat. Where did you buy it?' I couldn't resist making a play for his vanity.

'At an emporium,' he answered lazily; the side of his mouth closest to me a couple of teeth are gone from the pink plastic gum.

'What about yer coat? Must 'uv worked pretty 'ard for that.'

'I am not a prostitute. Though at the time my husband gave it to me I was admittedly a wife.'

'Don't think much of we men. And I never went much on you libbers.'

'I was never in need of liberation. I knew what I wanted and went out and got it.' (Dishonest statement coming from one who doesn't yet know why she is where. But the man provoked me.)

He began again at the next lights. 'Reckon you take it easy nowadays.'

'I'm kept busy.'

'Reckon they bring their kids for nanna to keep an eye on.'

'There are no *grand*children – thank God!'

'I'm with yer there. But the women seem to go along with it. A string of snotty little kids lets the neighbours see you've made a contribution.'

'I like to think I've made a contribution without benefit of snot. Oh, I know all about squalor – I've been up to my ears in it at times, but squalor of a grander range.'

We were sliding past houses and gardens, and railings, railings.

The railings reminded me to ask, 'Were you ever in gaol?'

He winced, and the gooseflesh stood out amongst the hairs on the muscular arms. 'What a thing to ask an honest man!' He aimed a short sharp burst of spit at the road.

The passenger carries on. 'I never was. All my crimes went undetected. Even a murder or two . . .'

'Cripes! I took yer for a lady of wealth and status – in that snazzy coat.'

'It's the snazzy ones who commit some of the worst crimes – the murders that are overlooked.'

'You've got something there. But you must 'uv done somethun between committing the murders that was overlooked. You say you keep busy. What 'uv yer been busy at?'

'I'm an artist.'

'You don't say! Go in for a bit of art work meself at weekends. Course I don't let on to the blokes. Dunno why – don't do no 'arm to anybody.'

'Art can be almost a worse crime than living.'

'Eh?'

'That's what I'm trying to decide. I've got to discover – by writing out – acting out my life – the reason for my presence on earth. Doesn't that sound reasonable?'

'No way! It's the nuttiest proposition I ever heard. Mind you, I'm not suggestin' . . .'

'Actually you are, but I'm not holding it against you.'

'What are you writing, any'ow?'

'That won't be known till after I'm dead.'

'Well, which programme do you act on?'

'I act live.'

'Never been to a live play. Wouldn't 'ave the nerve.'

'I'll see they give you tickets. When I asked you to take

me to the Westpac Bank, Martin and George, it was one
of those subterfuges people adopt. I was afraid to tell you
I wanted to go to the Sand Pit theatre. Know it?'

'Heard about it. Yairs. Full of Commies and poofs.'

As I rummage through my bag for money, 'I was never
a Commie. Could be a poof. Might ask you up if you ever
bring me home.'

I hand him the fare. Slightly lower my eyelids. I smile
at him. I know the tips of my teeth will be looking transparent. He takes the money, but ignores the implications.

'What name do you write – act under? Might have seen
it in the *Telegraph*.'

'Princess Alexandra Xenophon.'

'Jesus! What's all this?'

'You're not surely above a tip?'

'In a democratic country – and from a bloody phoney
princess! If it was Di, say – or Alexandria . . .'

'You needn't have qualms. I swiped the tip – the fare
too – from my daughter's housekeeping money. It may be
some consolation to know I'm as dishonest as yourself –
and many others.'

I watch him as he drives off. Have I recruited a witness
for the prosecution in the trial I must face sooner or later?

Inwardly athletic, outwardly exhausted, I mount the
theatre steps.

Today and the days which follow we spend putting the
play together (democratically) from our shorthand notes
and X-ray plates of the fatal diseases most of us are suffering from. A girl in specs insists on playing a foetus '. . . an
only too obvious starting point . . .' A lady with a ginger
moustache sees herself as an urban guerrilla. 'This is a play

of action, surely – of revolution – and no action is possible today without urban guerrillas. Whoever presses the button – and whenever – the urban guerrilla is the catalyst.'

I am surprised to find I can keep so quiet. They don't yet know what they have on their hands – all these foetuses and gingery guerrillas. If it hadn't been for my chinchilla, I might not have existed. The coat draws a few snide glances. I hear myself referred to as Old Possum and the Cat Lady. In the beginning I thought of dumping the coat at my down-market end of the dressing room, but it is so cold in the dark, badly ventilated theatre, I decide to keep it hugged round my body.

Even during the coffee-cum-bladder break when we go outside and sit on the steps in the unnatural sunlight, I hug my coat and it hugs me. The young things around me lap up the filthy stuff from the urn. One group in particular huddles together sharing a joint while discussing motivation and structure. My friend Dara brings me a cup of urn coffee which I refuse with my most charismatic smile. Dara is one of those Russian toys weighted at the bottom which you can't knock over, fortunate Dara. There is Lin too. She shares with us slivers of chewy Chinese duck. We are our own little enclave, ethnic outcasts in a colonial democratic society. When it is time to go back inside, Dara and Lin shore me up, unnecessarily I should add, one of them under each of my armpits, like a pair of human crutches.

Trevor, one of our many authors, and perhaps director in default of one, is discussing what he sees as an effective scene. His eyes flicker in our direction. 'There are these three peasant women – Sino-Something – Russian who knows what – and a Greco-Turkish whatever. Y'know? But above all, *peasants*.' Lin and Dara accept the shadowy definitions of what they are expected to be. 'You, Alex, must know all about the Turkish thing.'

I don't reply. I only smile. The others, that is the foetuses and urban guerrillas, are looking at me, not because they understand, but because they foresee the humiliation of some kind of old phoney amateur the management has roped in to lend authenticity to an unimportant scene.

'Now,' says Trevor, 'you three peasants are doing your laundry on the banks of a stream. Sloshing your linen against the stones, rubbing it against the washing boards.'

Obediently, Lin and Dara are doing just this (they have both been to NIDA).

'Get me, Alex?'

I must have been hesitating, lost in the mists of memory, gathering together strands from the past focusing in my mind's eye, scenting cleanliness in my nostrils.

'Oh, *yes!*'

It all floods back. Our old Smaragda. Our darling who held me in her arms aboard the destroyer after we escaped the flames, and who vanished mysteriously soon after we reached the mouth of the Nile, the Pharos, and comparative safety promised by banker relatives.

Oh *yes* . . .

Soon I am sloshing the sheets around, over the stones, rubbing them against the corrugated board with all the strength of my aged peasant body. The stream courses down the slope from a spring higher in the hills. Hands cracked and reddened by lye in the crude soap we are using in rubbing and scrubbing. My neatly braided plaits tremble. My thin lips are parted in a smile over toothless gums. A virgin smile. I am the virgin who has given birth to my own and suckled other people's children. Ingrained virtue in every wrinkle of my wizened face. Wrongdoing is beyond my scope. I am pure as this sheet I have laundered.

In a sudden burst of vanity I hold this glistening banner against the light.

'You wouldn't see a whiter sheet anywhere in Australia.'

Trevor laughs, vindicated. 'That's right, old dear! A dazzler!'

He comes forward, grasps by the shoulder, not Xenophon's Smaragda, not myself Alex Gray, but a person he's taken a gamble on, and fitted successfully into their jigsaw of a play.

Everyone is relieved now that we have run through this excisable (sub-subtext) scene and can get on with the contentious issues. Should the Urban Guerrillas enter through the auditorium or parachute down from the roof? Should the play end with the Bomb or an aftermath of ash?

The Foetus is coping badly with a fit of the sulks or pre-menstrual pains.

According to the rules we shall soon be leaving the theatre for the night. Going home. The idea appals me. The theatre has become my home. How can I face the ghosts from the past which intrude nightly from the Park and lurk in every cupboard in the house? For that matter, the living ghost my daughter.

I rub diffidently against Trevor. Couldn't I spend the night here? I'm not on best terms with my family.

Trevor is all *bonhomie* this evening, somebody has promised to sleep with him. 'If it's martyrdom you're after!' He even fetches a camp-bed and sets it up outside the lavatories.

Martyrdom? Haven't I got my chinchilla? And soon

there will be silence. There is nothing as silent as a theatre when the play is done and the actors have gone their various ways.

I lie on my camp-bed, its bones at war with mine, outside the pizzling lavatories, in the almost dark. The almost silence. It is the dark of moon-washed oilskins, the dark of skittering cockroaches.

'Glabrous' is a word which possesses me. I mean to explore, taste it thoroughly when I get back to my writing. 'My glabrous love ...' my lovers, with the exception of Onouphrios the monk at Ayia Ekaterini, have been more or less smooth. 'The glabrous dark' ... in this deserted theatre it is far from hairless. Where the chinchilla has fallen back from my legs, I can feel the little hairy haunches which accompany the slither of a tail. A little red eye is trying to outstare me. It won't. Or possibly it will. I claw through the bag for my fountain-pen torch, which I carry for following the lines of a script or names in a programme – or to examine my neighbour's wrists. So important, wrists. One day I might try tying love-knots on a neighbour's wrist.

Not now. Oh, cold, shivery, cockroach-skittering, rat-infested dark. I make for the bar by instinct. The rat has preceded me. I see his little red eye. I hear him chomping on carrot cake and quiche. We have become familiars. When by accident my hand touches his naked tail dangling from the edge of the bar-top, he does not withdraw.

Oh God, I am not afraid of a mere rat when I have stood up to some of the dinosaurs of disaster. I go round focusing the eye of my torch. The salt flowers of a Margarita are blooming in my mind. Bugger the salt, the lemon, the tequila is what my shrivelled tongue is letching after. I would lick the tail of any rat prepared to illuminate the bottle.

Ahhhh!

I put away what I wouldn't like to reckon in barmaid's business tots. What the hell! I am crashing through, into a world of diamond splinters. Another gluggle. What about the bottle, the management? Fill it with water against the day of reckoning. The jug bounces, crashes, adding its lesser splinters to the incorporeal jabs which have broken out in my mind.

I crawl back on all fours in the direction of the camp-bed, the chinchilla, the never-silent lavatories. I lie awaiting dawn and judgment.

Somewhere through the dawn light I can hear – no *smell* Hilda brewing up in the kitchen. Sometimes when in a good temper she offers me a cup from her brew. It is this Roma special caramel blend she buys at the Junction when she abandons McDermott principles. The cups are those transparent white ones she gets for free according to the extent of her purchases. She tells me the cups are art deco. The addict's lip-print stays for ever on the transparent white of the free art-deco cup.

I offer up a prayer to the perfume my daughter has distilled. If you were to melt the pigeon's blood ruby Harry Gray snitched from behind a lattice in Lahore and brought back to Sydney Australia, it would rise plumed and lan-guorous as the aroma from Hilda's coffee.

Is there any point in my going down and appealing to the charity in her?

I don't. The grey strands of morning have begun to drift through the foyer and my splintered head. They mingle with the pizzling of the lavatories. Later on the actress/

servant will arrive to slop around the lavatories, ignore the incurable graffiti, and animate the sludge in the coffee urn.

I turn away from the abyss of light opening amongst the crumpled programmes and trampled quiche. My flickering eyelids are frail blinds against such a glaze.

Hang on to something. Must. Think glabrously. The glabrous shaman. No such thing. But the word could be accommodated. Some. Where.

They tell you to keep a notebook. That's where all such splinters and masturbatory devices are stored. Indispensable after death, for the parasite students and academics who eat out your liver and lights – your *heart*.

No point. It's all in the Memoirs. Too much of it.

I must resign myself. Patrick will be the spirit guide at the great seance. I respect him as far as anybody, including oneself, can be respected.

The days are piling up. Costumes. At the Sand Pit they prefer the trademarks of authenticity. A piss-stained fly. Armpitted T-shirts. A ball dress on which food has added to the pattern. The Foetus is in despair over an enormous Winterhalter hat designed for the Empress Eugénie she can't very well adapt to the characters she will play. (Shall I offer to wear it for her as myself? They can't expect me to stay put as a peasant throughout.)

Photographs. The real *grainy* stuff for a way-out group. Show up every pimple, blackhead, mean little hair in a guerrilla lady's ginger moustache.

I am not much chop in the circumstances. If only they stopped to consider what I might have to offer. Here I am, the Empress Alexandra of Nicaea, Byzantium, the lot. My stomacher alone – cabuchon emeralds, pigeons' blood rubies the size of pigeons' eggs, with stones of lesser value but greater mystical significance. The black scarab from an Egyptian tomb. Over my head an agate circlet shimmering like a ring of grey water in some metaphysical dawn.

The photographers wander to and fro expressionlessly clicking a fortune away to celebrate this ephemeral event. If one of them dropped to my presence I'd make him Press Photographer of the Year with one click. Perhaps it is my mouth that puts them off. Its crimson has overflowed the bounds I set it with my eyebrow pencil. Too emotional a life leads to a shaky hand.

Click, click. It is over. They relax and share a joke, a cup of urn sludge with younger lips. Pale, but juicy slugs sleepily smiling a confidence they don't possess this side of the sheets.

Pfui to all leotarded sluts! Trevor drags me back into the shadows. He is always dragging me in some direction, an additional crutch to those provided by my faithful supporters Dara and Lin. Is Trevor afraid I may let him down? Or does he perhaps have tickets on me? Try tying the love knots in the hairs of Trevor's wrist. I look at him as closely as I can, to trap that moment of recognition. He is looking nowhere unless at the photographer with the blackest clone moustache.

Oh pfui oh fuck. Yawn yawn. My feet are aching. My empty stomach is regurgitating a ribbon of sour wind.

Everybody is arriving for opening night at the Sand Pit. When I say Everybody I don't mean the lady who stays home baking sponges for the grandkiddies, or the bloke who simply stays at home because what has leaving it got to offer. When I say Everybody I mean all those who are contributing to life by being where the cameras are. It's expected of us. What use would Emily Dickinson have been keeping to her room with her supraterrestrial pre-occupations? The media wouldn't have stood for that, they would have dragged her down to ground level amongst the plastic and adulteries, and bugger her grain of sand.

Nothing is honest that isn't explicit. Shit is no longer a dirty word, it's a realistic expletive. Now that the press has brought us together, now that we know one another intimately, in bed and out, at breakfast, dinner, and on the dunny, we have nothing more to expect, nothing to fear. So why are we afraid, particularly of one another?

I, who have no need of any media bounty, remain afraid. I have been everywhere. I know all. Am all, I am the Creator. Perhaps for that very reason I am afraid of what I have let loose, of what I have created.

So on opening night at the Sand Pit, when Everyone is here, I keep going apart, telling my beads, swinging my *komboloyi*, looking for advice which won't be forthcoming. When I return inevitably to face the auditorium, I see the faces of those who will sit in judgment on the Panto-crator.

The lights dim. I catch sight of the *S.M.H.* perched at a safe enough distance from actual proceedings. His ears are unmistakable, those of an anaemic bat, its pallor fluor-escent.

Who is with whom is the question in the ranks of regimented denim. Watch for the protective arm. She's wanked her way to academic approval. She's landed her part in his next play. Blobs of black here and there from Cabinet Ministers doing their duty by the Yartz. Luscious young women in expensively dowdy model clothes glance fleetingly at their own faces to see how much the glass reveals of their afternoon activities. Lovely faces, the blowsier for illicit love. Love-bitten necks and shoulders. Flesh boiling over. In other rows prim little nipples not above giving their all in the name of Aust. Lit. To thin-shanked hungry wife-ridden men – or voracious women. Forget the means in a mean world, it's the end that matters.

The twittering slowly ceases as in a fowl shed or aviary at dusk. Are we beginning? Or have we begun? Most likely we never stopped running through this waking dream of my life. Have the three peasant women gone through their act sloshing their washing around on the stones in Asia Minor, China, Siberia, or anywhere else? The audience give no sign of having witnessed it. Too insignificant of course, for those whose smoked salmon and Veuve Clicquot still rumble in their stomachs. Or perhaps our Smaragda never existed except as a figment of my prolific mind.

In the bio-box a red sun has risen through the smoke of the unkindled fires of this non-revolutionary revolutionary play. What will move an audience? They laugh as the Urban Guerrillas parachute down from the girders. All these gingery liberated ladies might be no more than autumn leaves. A patron awakes in a midway row, far less important than her social importance demands. She explores her back hair. Farther down, a sigh from one who returns her hand between her escort's bursting thighs, and snuggles up.

What can I do? I am waiting to perform some act expected of me in the context of a play, dream, my own life – whichever. I can see the Critic sidling on his intolerably uncomfortable Sand Pit seat, itching to fling a subtext into the arena. I reach a point where I believe the cue will never be forthcoming. I must act of my own free will.

I do. Suddenly a spot is aimed at the platform on which I shall perform. There is that smell of light dusting down boards for the Great Moment. I step forward. So many hands reach out to restrain me I might be surrounded by a whole mythology of Hindu gods and goddesses.

The audience is galvanised in row after row of denim chic, with here and there a drift of froth, caught on a reef of ministerial black.

I open the mouth which has overflowed the boundaries set by an eyebrow pencil. 'This is Dolly Formosa speaking to the Happy Few.' They are with me in a flash, because no one can ever resist belonging to the Happy Few even in these days when élitism has been voted out. My Happy Few are waiting moist-eyed for the message.

I don't pander to them. I have assumed the form, mime the motions of a huge predatory bird threatening any bones they may have left unpicked in their hunger for fame, titles, and Orders. Oh, those Orders! Ladies protect the juicier parts of their anatomy.

What should have appeared menacing and tragic, suddenly becomes so farcical I let out a great quark of laughter, at the same time bringing from behind my back Hilary Gray's service revolver, and without taking aim, firing at random into this covey of defenceless game which might have been put up by beaters for their Sovereign's pleasure at a Royal shoot.

Hit by a blank, a victim falls in the third row. A full-throated scream. His student doxy bends over him to assess the damage.

I fire here and there. I aim in the direction of the Critic, but already his bat's wings are carrying him into the night as he heads for Neptune's Cave.

A further sprinkling of blanks produces a heart attack, a crypto-corpse. Screams and sirens. Paddy-wagons and ambulances.

The lights go up on the general shambles. About the middle of the house a figure sits it out, her face the shape and colour of a white enamelled bedpan. Her laughter resounds so madly it suggests she may have grasped the reason for the exercise. In the centre of the pan-shaped face she has painted a crimson cupid's bow to match my own overflowing mouth. I aim at the cupid's bow and score a bull's eye. It does not stop the woman's maniacal laughter. It is louder than ever, only with a slight crackling at its enamelled edges. I fire and fire, till silence. My blanks are spent.

Some person of authority has been edging this way and that all this while, forwards and retreating, forwards and retreating. Now he springs and yanks me by an arm.

'Steady on, Craig – no, Trevor – or is it Wayne? You could very easily break a bone.'

He runs me as far as the office.

I am not surprised to find Falkenberg waiting for me. I hold out my arms for our embrace, and am soon snugly encased in the familiar canvas sleeves.

'A lifetime is never as long as it seems. Or would you say it is?'

I smile at him, and might have put up a hand to arrange my hair if I had not been so neatly trussed.

I sit in my cell, seemingly part of a murmurous hive below ground level. Ancient, honey-coloured stone walls broken by strata of equally ancient grey cement, fragments of oyster shell embedded in it. There are no chains, but there is no need since I am wearing my jacket. I have my chair, a truckle bed, and a covered pail for my convenience.

I sit and wait. It is not so very different from the outside world because life in whatever surroundings or circumstances is a series of variations on the theme of waiting.

My gaoler is Nurse XYZ. I have heard her name, but have blotted it out of my mind for fear I might remember it in a more enlightened future. There is also her male counterpart, Swan, who so far has displayed a few of the more human qualities.

Nurse has a beautiful skin, bluish white at the nape of her neck where the black hair is gathered up and bundled with help of a comb under the cap. Her calves bulge in their black stockings above the sturdy shoes. The shoes should be cloven like a bull's hooves. The face ... I must not invoke it.

Her remarks, almost always offensive, are propelled from between those thick lips, bubbling with spite. 'All you high-born ladies - if you *are*, outside of your imagination - think that because you've been spoilt at home you're going to get the same treatment here. No, *ma'am!* as they say Princess Margaret expects. We're all equals at Bonkers Hall.'

Her laughter is a rumbling contralto which agitates the full breasts inside her grey cotton uniform.

'Costive are yer? Open wide. If I had the key to the dispensary I'd dose the lot of yez night and morning with a lovely tot of castor oil.'

When I fail to make the pail in time, and mess the seat, she grabs a handful of paper. 'Know what it is? If you don't you will,' as she pastes my face, back and forth, 'Shit! Shit!'

When her fury has subsided she calls in Swan with an enamel basin and washer, and leaves me to him. We hear her stamping up the stone stairs to a higher level.

'What would we do without the males, eh?' Swan has a strong arm above a limp wrist; and a somewhat leery smile under his Tartar moustache.

When he has finished cleaning me up, he lifts my skirt and sticks two fingers inside my vagina.

'Can't say I'm not a friend, love.'

His eyes grow round with malicious surprise as he removes the fingers and holds them up for our mutual inspection. 'Waddayerknow – *rust!*'

I am left at last to the silence of my cell, cleansed of my last film of vanity, but with a stench which will probably never leave my nostrils.

I am visited by the Superintendent; a gentleman of marked military appearance.

'Yes, Colonel. No. Colonel. Yes, Colonel Hackett, nobody can say as Mrs Gray isn't doing nicely.'

'Does she behave herself, Nurse?'

The hawkish expression, the pale blue eyes, the fine red veins, the grey moustache, only half believe in the questions it is his duty to ask.

Nurse simpers her way through a benevolent character role. 'Oh yes, you can't say milady isn't a gentle old soul.'

What else? Trussed as I am in my canvas jacket.

'Think she might do without this, Nurse?' tweaking at my sleeve.

'Well, Colonel. We might try. Yairs, we can only try.'

She comes back after the Colonel has returned to the

tantalus he keeps in his quarters. The bull's muzzle is snorting as she unties the tapes. My arms are freed from the blind sleeves. For what purpose? They are feeble as seedlings raised in a cellar.

'Just you try to create, my girl, and you'll be back in this before tea's up!'

She leaves me. I remain seated on my chair. At one level of my consciousness I have flung myself at the nape of her blue-white neck. I have sunk my teeth in the milky skin. She can't throw me off. Her screams call for help and vengeance, but she can't be heard from the depths of a purgatory to which we are both condemned.

I don't ask for Justice, only justice.

Swan brings the bowl of sedated slops we are served as an evening meal.

'A free woman! That's progress, isn't it?'

XYZ must be losing her grip. The Colonel is showing more concern. On one occasion he brings my first visitor. Nurse stands by, breathing audibly. Her opinion is no longer sought.

'What do you think?' the Colonel asks the visitor in undertone.

He answers in an aged, dusty voice.

Is this my adversary grown old? The Falkenberg with whom in a former life I longed to grapple, beak to beak, breast to breast, wing-tip slashing wing-tip – in short, hatred matching hatred – or love. (An admission I would never make to Patrick or Hilda; they wouldn't believe.)

Evidently he is this old, wrinkled, pockmarked creature who murmurs, 'Yes, vee heff nossing to lose. It is a risk vee must tek.'

Is this caricature of a reffo the demon who cast a spell on Alex Gray, who wooed her in vibrant tones with lines from masters like Madács, Arany, and Goethe, and when he had won her over, passed sentence on her?

'Wasn't it called *The Tragedy of Man?*'

'Faht?' He looks so alarmed I want to hold him in my arms and soothe his fears.

Colonel Hackett clears his throat. He is here for professional reasons only. A wave of hysteria and sentimental recollection is rising round his colleague and this infernal woman. Well, the Superintendent has no intention of getting caught in the undertow.

'On your recommendation, Professor, we'll try it.'

XYZ is blowing like a whale.

I am reduced to snivelling self-pity: I must sound an imbecile, but the Colonel is used to idiocy. 'All I ask for ... a roomful of light ... some writing-paper ... and a pen.'

At mention of the pen, the Colonel sees a sharp object. A risk.

They leave me. Professor Falkenberg does not look back. At the end of his life, he may have acted imprudently.

So I am restored to the living. In the beginning I can scarcely keep my balance in this world of light. If I sit, I float horizontally like the moored boats I see through my window. The window is barred, but the bars do not prevent the interchange of sensation between myself, trees, the boats floating in this radiant backwater. If I try to wrest myself from the horizontal and attempt the vertical position normal to waking human beings, I am threatened with toppling unless I reach out and support myself on the nearest piece of furniture.

In this cube of expanding and contracting light (I no longer think of it as a cell) I have the standard truckle bed, a chair, and most important, the table on which are laid four piles of unblemished foolscap. And two ball-point pens, one black, one red.

Now that I am free to write, shall I ever dare begin to sort out my disordered thoughts? It is a frightening prospect. I sit with my hands back to back, held tightly between my knees. I reel if I look inside my churning abyss of a mind. But I must MUST remain in the vertical position. Reason's posture is vertical, like Hilda's spinal column. If Patrick were here he could guide me. No. I must do it myself. Patrick guide! Patrick cannot guide himself, that's why he's taken to carrying a walking stick.

I I I ... that's how I began, how I covered all those sheets of paper stashed away in the priest hole, overflowing drawers and suitcases in the house above Centennial Park.

I take up the black ball-point and start myself hobbling stumbling along the topmost line of this sheet of white foolscap in my hygienic room. Too hygienic perhaps. I am brought to a full ● Perhaps there was never anything there and I only imagined it. I throw down the sharp object of which Colonel Hackett had his doubts. He may have been right. I could have aborted my ego somewhere back along the line. I take up the horrid red ball-point and dig a deep, bloody trench from top to bottom of the innocent sheet. Through my own lack of skill I shall remain sterile for ever after.

Oh God, prevent me ... Save me from the jacket ...

Enter Mrs Sieveking. I seem to have met her in some other play. I forget which. She is wearing civilian clothes, a pattern of big cinnamon and fuchsia flowers, a choice which no doubt pleases her. She takes my hand and we sit together on the edge of the bed. She is a socio-something or other, to do with rehabilitation.

'I am here to help you,' she tells me. 'We must all help each other mustn't we? Then we may find our troubles not as bad as somebody else's.'

The grains of beige powder tremble as the wrinkles round her mouth open and close. I accept her intentions as kindly.

'Are you a mature woman, Mrs Sieveking?'

'I hope so. Like yourself, Mrs Gray.'

'How old are you?'

She hesitates. 'Fifty-six,' she says, 'more or less.'

I can't help noticing all those blank sheets of paper on the table.

'At least at your age, Mrs Gray, you don't have to worry. You've overcome it.'

'But I worry more and more. How old do you think I am?'

'I'd say at a guess seventy-five.' She smiles her kindliest beige smile.

'Sometimes I feel I'm marked down to seven or eleven.' A wind is rising, jostling the boats tethered in their blue field. 'If I'm not an aborted foetus in a bottle.'

'We must have faith ...' a methodical or baptismal mumbling.

She has fetched a nurse, not XYZ, a long thin one with no chin. She gives me an injection.

When I wake, if you can call it that, there is a lesser confusion of voices and faces. I am wrapped, not in the customary jacket, but a blanket. I cannot see what I am wearing. Will they have forgotten my regalia? I detect the accents of Colonel Hackett fresh from the tantalus he keeps for distinguished visitors, but chiefly for himself in his coming and going amongst the committed insane. I believe I catch a glimpse of the wrinkly, pocked mask time has forced Falkenberg into wearing. He is watching through fearful slits to see if there is any value left in one of his most profitable meal tickets.

The men of action are of greater interest. They always are in the beginning. Professional males. In their laundered shirts, shoulder tabs, caps stiffly peaked. None of your denim pretends. The ambulance men are both reddish gingery freckled. I smell the after-shave from jaws freshly glazed.

'What is your name?'

'Tom.'

They are both Toms.

I stroke an arm from the smooth biceps through the gingery fuzz down as far as the wedding ring. They are both, we are all, ringed.

The after-shaved professionals are briefly replaced by the sweaty police carrying Saint Bernadette down from the mountains on the stretcher improvised out of saplings and an overcoat. We were all praying.

I try to remember a prayer, and fail, as the after-shaves, the Toms, lift me from the bed where the professional stretcher has been resting.

A nurse is hovering over me. It is the chinless one who gave me the injection. She is wearing a little cape for the journey and clutching a board with some papers bulldogged to it. Nurse Elvers, I seem to remember hearing.

'Where are they taking us, Nurse?'

'To St Damien's.' Her voice has acquired overtones of holiness.

'Why?'

'You are sick. And your family specially asked for St Damien's.'

'They're not Catholic.'

'No, but it's handy for visits.'

In the ambulance Elvers has seated herself beside my stretcher, clutching her board of bulldogged papers. Her bony knees almost touch her chin.

'What have you done with mine?' I ask.

'Your what?'

'The papers on my writing table.'

'But there was nothing on them. Except a line. A red line.'

'That's right. Patrick might want to see it. All is grist. He doesn't let a shopping list slip through his net.'

'Patrick Who?'

'The writer. Haven't you heard of him?'

'Never!'

'He'd appreciate that. He's sick of writers. Of me – if he weren't so polite. He's sick of himself. Literature, as they call it, is a millstone round his neck.'

We are stopping and starting, bumping over many bridges.

'What is your other name, Elvers?'

'Why?'

'Names are important. I can never have enough of them myself. A freshly acquired name gives me a fresh leave of life.'

'If you must know – my name is Ilma.'

'Why "Ilma"?'

'My mother was in service when she started her preg-
nancy. She fainted while waiting at table – handing the
Brussels sprouts – at a ladies' luncheon – in the Eastern
Suburbs. When they revived her, and got her up from
amongst the sprouts, she told her employer, "I'm not ill,
ma'am. Only a slight nausea. I'll be all right in a jiffy." But
they sacked her, afraid it might happen again. ". . . not ill,
ma'am, not ill . . ." She heard herself as she went home on
the tram. Like a clock ticking in her ears. That's how she
came to call me "Ilma".'

The ambulance was swirling recklessly.

'Don't know why I'm telling you this.'

'It passes the time.'

'That's right. We're nearly there.'

'And then you decided to nurse the mad.'

'Don't say that. I call it "deranged" – and between ourselves, who isn't?'

Ilma Elvers and I were enjoying a cosy giggle as we
drew up outside Admission.

The last I saw of real life was Ilma's non-chin before
Sister Philomena officially sedated me.

Notes

p. 148 *prana*: life force

p. 166 *komboloyi*: a string of beads derived from the Roman
rosary. Regrettably referred to by Anglo Saxons as
'worry beads'

p. 169 Neptune's Cave: late-night restaurant patronised by
theatre people

p. 173 Madács: Hungarian epic poet
Arany: Hungarian epic poet

Epilogue

'We'd better face her.'

'Give her time to settle in.'

I accept her daughter's decision.

'They'll send for us if there's a genuine crisis. You know Mother. Her life has been a series of crises.'

She didn't have to tell me.

Some way back Hilda had started to fossick for the papers. The house was stuffed with them. Under the eaves in what has been referred to as the priest hole. Crammed into drawers, so full they refused at first to open. Under the mattress. In old mouldy suitcases. Each batch with its attendant smell, from oppressive perfume to disgusting stench.

Often I found myself wishing: if only a fire ... But I knew I would never escape Alex. If her papers went up in smoke, her life was mine historically, personally, and if I cared to admit, creatively.

During this period of waiting for what we used to refer to as the End, I spent most of my time at the house on the Park, while keeping as far away from Hilda as I possibly could. She was not herself. She was overcome by uncharacteristic lethargy or downright sloth.

'One day I'll get down to cleaning up. But not yet. There doesn't seem any point till a person dies and the will is read. At least we've got her papers together. We know she is leaving you those. She always expected you would do the right thing by her literary remains. As Hal and I do too. You are so discreet.'

Curious how others pin their expectations on those they have known all their lives without knowing. Only Alex really knew, because she might have created me, and I her. We were both remote from her almost non-existent son Hal, and her actual daughter Hilda. Or so we thought.

It was only later that I got to know the real Hilda. Perhaps Alex had known all the time and bequeathed Hilda, along with the papers recording our actual and created lives as a kick in the pants, or monstrous joke.

The call from the hospital blasted the house apart. We should come if we wanted to pay our last respects to Mrs Alex Gray. She seemed to be expecting us.

It was an evening of drizzle interspersed with sunshine, neither cold nor warm, clammy rather, like a sweaty sheet in the aftermath of a nightmare.

Hilda roused herself and rang for a taxi.

The cab slid alongside the fence, the driver tooting. The man was neither young nor old, firmly fleshed of thigh and arm, wearing dark glasses, a cynical expression, and Digger's hat.

I gave our destination as St Damien's.

We slid along, past houses and gardens which in all these years I hadn't bothered to people, and on the other side, railings, railings.

The driver was vibrating with suppressed questions. Finally, 'Where I picked you up – isn't that the home of the actress?'

'Yes. Or was . . . she's very ill.'

'Never saw 'er act. Any'ow, on stage.'

I had no desire to encourage him, Hilda even less.

Such a short distance, we were there almost as soon as we started. Relatives were leaving and arriving, carry-all in hand, or else a bunch of drooping flowers. Only we were empty-handed.

As I paid the fare, the driver swivelled in his seat and looked full at me, the cynical smile, Digger's hat and dark glasses.

'Good luck. And kind regards to Princess Thingummy, the actress.'

I saw that most of his teeth had broken off from the pink plastic gums. His grin was positively ferocious.

He drove off as we went inside.

At the duty desk where Hilda inquired, 'Mrs Alex Gray – her daughter and a close friend,' the Sister smiled, was it knowingly? 'Oh yes, she's expecting you.' Expectation at every turn made it unnerving.

The Sister led us down the corridor, our clattering foot-steps more substantial than our bodies.

Silence broken by distant laughter, coughing, and at times, the sound of someone fetching up the dregs of a lifetime.

We were led into quite a large room where three elderly moribund women were lying.

Out of deference to our relationship with one of the three, the Sister drew curtains around the bed, providing a degree of privacy.

'Mrs Gray, dear,' the Sister spoke loud, 'your daughter and', emphasising it, '*friend*.'

She smiled and left us to deal with the situation.

Alex did not look at us. 'Where have all the nuns gone?'

'I noticed one on the way in.'

I offered this fatuous remark as we drew up chairs either side of the bed.

'But there ought to be lots,' she mused in a faint, colourless voice one could scarcely hear.

'Nuns – Valkyries – bats with blood dripping from their jaws – as they flew overhead – in the days when I was a prospective Saint.'

Hilda was agonising on the brutal hospital chair.

Alex did not seem or did not want to notice us.

The sockets had shrunk, around eyes which those expecting the convention of an Oriental Greek had never believed in. The blue had grown foggy with age and illness.

'Yes,' she murmured, 'I was nuts about nuns. Not so much for monks or priests.'

It was a relief to be curtained off from the world. The three of us sat in what amounted to a translucent cell. At the centre this ancient creature, the darkened arms like writhing mangrove branches ending in twig claws, on one of which a wedding ring shone. Far more distressing the head, shrunk to a black skull, from which the eyes looked out at what one could not be sure.

She seemed to be on again about the nuns. 'My darling Bernadette ... Today there's too much jumping over the wall.'

Hilda could no longer contain herself. 'I'm sure every one of the young women caring for the patients in this hospital is as dedicated as any nun. And with nuns you run into mysticism. I wouldn't want a mystic counting my pills.'

The skull had not taken in any of this. The gnarled body made an effort and raised itself against the pillows.

I would have liked to help, but was struck powerless. I was hypnotised by what I saw as the moment when the last of human frailty makes contact with the supernatural.

'Is it this – then ...?' she whispered, whether in horror, or ecstasy.

The black skull fell back against the pillows, a trickle of garnet-coloured blood escaping from one corner of the mouth.

Hilda jumped up, her chair shrieking on the floor, as she tore aside one wall of the cell. 'Nurse – *Sister*, come please,' she shouted down the corridor.

As her cry reverberated, many figures seemed rushing at once. I followed Hilda, who retreated, hunched, retching, a handkerchief pressed to her mouth as though to staunch the life blood welling up in resistance to her mother's death.

Suspended in evening sunlight, we sat in a little room to one side of the desk. Voices of children from a park below. A blow-fly desperately dashing itself against the upper pane of a half-open window. We did not speak to each other. Neither of us had the strength to release the blowie. I don't know how long we were there. It was pointless to look at a watch.

When someone came squelching down the corridor in what sounded like sandshoes. This time it was a real nun. She wore a muslin veil tied at the back of her head and the impersonal smile of one sure of her vocation.

The smile was directed at us. 'Would you like to see her?' she asked.

How could she be so sure the dead woman was ours? But certainty was her trademark.

Hilda stood up. 'No, thank you – Sister. I'd rather remember my mother as I knew her.'

Certainty at this moment was not in Hilda's line. Her mouth made it obvious that her memories would be bitter ones.

She stamped across the springy carpet, and down the stairs.

As I almost caught her up, she hissed back over her shoulder. 'They send a nun to lead you to the body, to con you into coughing up money for the Church, on top of the hospital bills.' She was rigid to breaking point. 'Well it doesn't work where I'm concerned. I know too much to be taken in.'

One evening months later as we sat at the kitchen table, mopping up after our boiled eggs, Hilda said, 'I have a plan.'

The way she stabbed the shell with her spoon made me apprehensive.

'I've been thinking it would be a good idea if we visited some of those places which played a part in her life – like Smyrna, Alexandria, Nisos. It might lay a few ghosts and help you in sorting out Mother's papers. Anyway, think it over, Patrick.'

In the weeks following the funeral and discussions with trustees, Hilda would collect me from my flat and return me there at night after a day spent at the house. But the last couple of weeks this routine had been broken. She packed a suitcase for me, closed the flat, and I moved to the house. Whether I approved or not, the arrangement had an air of permanence.

Tonight she said, 'Go upstairs – you must be tired – and I'll bring you your camomile.'

I did as I was told. She had aired and cleaned her mother's room. I should have been comfortable if the vast bed were not also the arena where Alex had spent so much of her life wrestling with the saints and demons wished into her at birth. Sensing their presence early on, I suppose I had encouraged her to cultivate them as an extension of my own creations.

Like most practically conceived tours, Hilda's plan for a return to those parts where her family had originated, and which had left their mark on her mother, did not work out too smoothly. I was too old, she too unrelenting. We were constantly losing our possessions, becoming separated from our baggage, missing air, rail, and boat connections, suffering from the customary indispositions like diarrhoea and indigestion. Almost everywhere Hilda found the sheets damp. Almost never was the plumbing adequate, or hot water forthcoming, even after she had made a scene to impress the management.

Nor were the ghosts laid. They still haunted the island of Nisos, where Aliki wrote her history of Bouboulina after settling in Metropolitan Greece at the end of the Second World War and the German Occupation. I met Cassianí the nun on a damp mountain track at dusk outside the church of Ayia Ekaterini. She hurried past, but I recognised her face surrounded by the dark kerchief. If I did not meet the monk Onouphrios I caught a whiff of his *fanella* at the entrance to the church. I distinctly heard the gunshot from at least one of the island's suicides.

I did not mention any of this to Hilda. She was too busy

carrying on her feud with the management over plumbing, hot water, and laundry at the hotel where we were staying at the little port.

One evening she said, as we wrestled with our muscular *brizoles*, 'I shall be glad when we leave for Italy. Italians are far more civilised than Greeks. And there won't be any family connections. We can enjoy ourselves looking at great art and eating deliciously cooked pasta.'

Such was her certainty she patted the back of my hand.

Italy ... From the start we realised she was full of menace for those in no way connected with her. As we strolled one evening beside the Bay of Naples, a bikie rode along-side the kerb and grabbed the shoulder bag of a man walk-ing a few yards ahead. The owner hung on to his bag and was dragged face down along the gritty pavement. The unsuccessful thief at last made off leaving his victim lying stunned, his pulped face scarcely human, more like a juicy nectarine ground almost beyond recognition on the floor of a truck on its way from the market.

Hilda hurried me away from what she decided was none of our business.

Again, in Rome, while exploring the Corso, a man dropped dead at our feet, following gunfire from behind the grille of one of those scruffy *palazzi*. Hilda reacted as in Naples, but on this occasion I could hardly accept it was none of our business. I distinctly heard the anarchic laugh-ter of Alex Gray from behind the *palazzo* grille.

Italy was obviously full of lawlessness and corruption, waiting to erupt in revolution, as a boil will swell and finally burst from its own pus.

Hilda said, 'The north will be more temperate,' adding

in spite of her principles, 'there's a measure of sanctity about the holy places of the north – Padua, Arezzo, Assisi.' She sighed. 'I long to see Assisi.' Then as though in an outburst against her defection from the rational norm, 'You can't expect sanctity in Rome, where one is asked to accept a whore's bed as the high altar of St Peter's.'

We had reached our hotel and she pushed me inside, afraid, I felt, we might be struck dead for her blasphemy in this holy city.

We were driven in the tourist bus to Assisi on a day of cold and drizzle. Hilda kept smiling at me, wistfully, which emphasised the little wrinkles in her face. It was as though she saw the journey as a pilgrimage, while at the same time asking forgiveness for a foolish lapse. I neither encouraged nor judged her. It was one of the days when I was thoroughly fed up with Hilda. I understood the mother's attitude to her daughter.

We arrived, and were plunged head first into the Basilica of San Francesco. It was easy to detach ourselves from our fellow tourists and the guide we had been allotted for the tour. Hilda strolled slowly letting it be seen that she appreciated Great Art. Nobody witnessing her performance would guess that she disapproved of the religious mythology which had inspired the paintings and frescoes. We were doing nicely when a Franciscan took up with us. He was probably there to keep an eye on suspicious characters intent on mutilation or theft. At first put out by our gratuitous guide, Hilda was finally charmed. Our Franciscan was most urbane, with cheeks polished to a high gloss, and intelligent eyes (if one hadn't been charmed, they might have appeared contemptuous). He spoke fluent English with a strong French accent. His even teeth bit crisply into every phrase he entered, as he pointed out works of art and memorabilia.

When we were finished and he led us out into a garden, Hilda turned to him like any citizen of Buffalo, 'Thank you', she said, 'for a truly great experience.'

The Franciscan might have winced if she had not followed it up with a smile which could have been disclaiming total innocence.

The sodden garden was disappointing. Not a bird in sight. They must have been shot by the Italian hunting classes. After the airlessness of the basilica it was shivery in the Saint's drizzled garden.

'And now', says the charmed Hilda to our charismatic guide, 'there is Santa Chiara. Can you point her out, and tell us how we get there?'

He did so. It was at the far end of Assisi, up a steep hill.

He hesitated, then confided, 'You know she's a fake, don't you? The mask – the head – they were manufactured by the nuns. They'd be Poor Clares indeed without such a source of revenue.'

Hilda turned away with what sounded like a shocked gasp.

Had he misjudged us? As a sophisticated Catholic, the Franciscan no doubt held the view that a pinch of scepticism is the salt which brings out the flavour in faith.

We started off up the hill to the church of Santa Chiara.

'A bitch – and French – there's nothing worse than a male bitch.' It could have been her mother speaking.

After the Franciscan ambience the church of Santa Chiara was ill-lit, gloomy. It presented a darker, more penitential aspect of faith. Hilda with her McDermott principles should have felt more at home, but I doubted it. She settled the collar of her top-coat closer round her neck, as though preparing for a confrontation she would have liked to avoid, and the final act of exorcism which one understood to be the object of our journey.

The two nuns who received us were dark-skinned, abject creatures, unlike the hearty freckled Irish of our Australian experience. They pointed out a few works of art, before offering, rather too hastily, to lead us into the Saint's presence in the crypt.

As far as I could see in this dim, candle-lit interior, Santa Chiara was reclining, a shrivelled mummy, in embroidered robes and a wreath of white everlastings, inside the traditional glass casket. The nuns crossed themselves and whispered to us pointlessly in Italian, extolling their saint's virtues, her miracles, and what have you.

I shuffled as close as I could to get a better view when I heard a choking sound and clattering behind me. Hilda had dropped her umbrella. Stooping to pick it up, she almost bumped heads with one of the nuns who had come to her assistance. So great was my interest in Santa Chiara I paid little attention to the mutterings and scrimmage behind me, and only vaguely realised that Hilda was making a getaway, as fast as she could, up the steps leading from the crypt. I finally realised what must have driven her. The candles, the incense, the glitter of embroideries, could not prevent me re-living a personal relationship with a barely human figure in another setting, life slipping from the dark skull as we watched. I would have sworn I could see a thread of garnet-coloured blood trickling from a corner of Santa Chiara's mouth.

By now I was ready to follow Hilda. I fumbled for my hip pocket and wallet. My stiff fingers could not have separated notes if they had tried. I scattered money in wads, with no thought for denomination. The nuns bent, almost grovelling in their gratitude for the generosity of this pious foreign benefactor.

Climbing out of the crypt, my walking stick was no longer a help, but an encumbrance.

Hilda was waiting in the Piazza del Comune where our guide had impressed on his flock that it should rejoin the bus. Regardless of the drizzle she was seated at one of the iron tables outside the Ristorante Italia, and was engaged in plastering her mouth with crimson. I had never seen her use make-up before, or only a smear of almost colourless salve, as for sore lips.

She looked at me, to defy any possible criticism. 'I found this lipstick in my bag. It must have been there for ages. Mother used to say, "If ever your morale needs a boost – if a lover or husband leaves you, for instance – buy yourself a new lipstick."'

I flopped down on one of the iron chairs. I felt too groggy to discuss the philosophy of lipstick.

Hilda got up and began feeling me. 'You're damp – *damp*, Patrick!' She arranged my scarf, turned up the collar of my overcoat. 'Better if we wait in the bus. You might catch a chill, darling.'

She helped me up the step, happier now that a reason for existence was restored to her. I hadn't the strength to resist.

Shortly after this we decided, or Hilda did, that we'd had enough of travel. Like most Australians who fancy themselves, we started hankering after our own Philistine environment and bourgeois habits, though we might not have confessed to it, of course.

Toiling up the steep path which meanders through the garden above the Park, Hilda was looking right and left. The unkempt grass, overgrown shrubs, particularly the monstera deliciosa, did not dent her apparent satisfaction with what she saw. 'All considered, everything is more or less in order.'

She was dragging the mammoth suitcase she had insisted on buying, 'Because we can share it and save ourselves a lot of trouble.' The suitcase was fitted with wheels, one of which had been wrenched off in the belly of a plane. Now as Hilda dragged the suitcase, it limped behind her, lopsided and grotesque. Leaning on my stick, I hobbled along, making a third.

At the top of the path, where we reached the corner of the house, two cats emerged from the jungle. 'Ah, Trifle! Tyger!' Hilda began to wheedle. They glared at us, mewed at us once or twice, and slunk into the next-door garden.

Inside the house, Hilda began barging round.

'Pfooh! Mildew!'

She flung open windows and doors to encourage draughts.

I took refuge in the kitchen, poured myself a dark-brown scotch and plonked myself down at the table.

'Home! Home!' she sang, opening the fridge and finding a carton of eggs the cat-minder neighbour must have left. 'One forgets how good people can be.'

I dread deafness, but wished I could have sealed my ears against any further dialogue.

After she had boiled and we had eaten our eggs, and she had swept shells and breadcrumbs into a 'Food City' plastic bag, she announced , 'We might never have been away.' Then, eyeing my glass, 'Not good for arthritis, darling, but we'll overlook it on a night like this.'

She stamped in the direction of our joint suitcase marooned in the hall. 'Shan't unpack tonight. I'll fish out your pyjamas – and toilet things – and finish tomorrow.'

While she was going about it I realised most forcibly that her mother had taken her revenge. Years ago Alex had said, 'I often think, Patrick, you should marry Hilda. I don't mean for sexual reasons. I'm sure my Hilda abhors the whole idea of the sexual act. But so that she could have something to look after. I'm no use to her, we know. But you, you silly old thing ...' She dwindled into a subdued but pointed laughter.

And this is what had happened. I was Hilda's possession: a bundle of sweaters, flannel shirts, down to the very last and most ignominious layer, those long-leg woollen underpants. To be dressed and undressed. Cosseted. Her thermometer always at the ready.

While I I – the great creative ego – had possessed myself of Alex Gray's life when she was still an innocent girl and created from it the many images I needed to develop my own obsessions, both literary and real.

If she had become my victim in those endless scribblings which I was faced at last with sorting out, I was hers through her authoritarian bigot of a daughter.

We were quits, oh yes, but never quit of each other.

Hilda came in. 'Your toothpaste's horribly mangled, darling. I'll have to give you a squeeze of mine.'

Notes

p. 185   Bouboulina: the pirate queen whose fleet rid the Aegean
of the Turk in the War of Independence
fanella: Greek undershirt

p. 186   *brizoles*: Greek rib chops, beef or veal